"Name your price, Miss Bennett," Cayo sugg... ...ke smoke and...

It was no won... ...less rivals went all wide-eyed and ... ...gave him whatever it was he wanted almost the very moment he demanded it. He was like some kind of corporate snake charmer.

But she wasn't one of his snakes, and she refused to dance to his tune—no matter how seductive. She'd been dancing for far too long, and this was where it ended. It had to. It would.

"I have no price," she said with perfect honesty. Once—yesterday—he could have smiled at her and she'd have found a way to storm heaven for him. But that had been yesterday. Today she could only marvel, if that was the word, at how naïve and gullible she'd been. At how well he'd played her.

"Everyone has a price."

And in his world, she knew, that was always true. Always. One more reason she wanted to escape it. Him.

Caitlin Crews discovered her first romance novel at the age of twelve. It involved swashbuckling pirates, grand adventures, a heroine with rustling skirts and a mind of her own, and a seriously mouthwatering and masterful hero. The book (the title of which remains lost in the mists of time) made a serious impression. Caitlin was immediately smitten with romances and romance heroes, to the detriment of her middle school social life. And so began her life-long love affair with romance novels, many of which she insists on keeping near her at all times.

Caitlin has made her home in places as far-flung as York, England, and Atlanta, Georgia. She was raised near New York City, and fell in love with London on her first visit when she was a teenager. She has backpacked in Zimbabwe, been on safari in Botswana, and visited tiny villages in Namibia. She has, while visiting the place in question, declared her intention to live in Prague, Dublin, Paris, Athens, Nice, the Greek Islands, Rome, Venice, and/or any of the Hawaiian islands. Writing about exotic places seems like the next best thing to moving there.

She currently lives in California, with her animator/comic book artist husband and their menagerie of ridiculous animals.

Recent titles by the same author:

THE MAN BEHIND THE SCARS
  (The Santina Crown)
IN DEFIANCE OF DUTY
HEIRESS BEHIND THE HEADLINES
PRINCESS FROM THE PAST

Did you know these are also available as eBooks?
Visit www.millsandboon.co.uk

A DEVIL
IN DISGUISE

BY
CAITLIN CREWS

MILLS
BOON

First published in Great Britain 2012
by Mills & Boon, an imprint of Harlequin (UK) Limited.
Harlequin (UK) Limited, Eton House, 18-24 Paradise Road,
Richmond, Surrey TW9 1SR

© Caitlin Crews 2012

ISBN: 978 0 263 89121 8

Harlequin (UK) policy is to use papers that are natural, renewable and recyclable products and made from wood grown in sustainable for-ests. The logging and manufacturing process conform to the legal environmental regulations of the country of origin.

Printed and bound in Spain
by Blackprint CPI, Barcelona

A DEVIL
IN DISGUISE

To Michelle Tadros Eidson for a few high finance clues, Jane Porter for two key backstory points that changed everything, and to Jeff Johnson for being the perfect husband to a crazed writer on deadline. Again.

CHAPTER ONE

"Of course you are not resigning your position," Cayo Vila said impatiently, not even glancing up from the wide expanse of his granite-and-steel desk. The desk loomed in front of a glorious floor-to-ceiling view over a gleaming wet stretch of the City of London, not that he had ever been observed enjoying it. The working theory was that he simply liked knowing that it was widely desired by others, that this pleased him more than the view itself. That was what Cayo Vila loved above all else, after all: owning things others coveted.

It gave Drusilla Bennett tremendous satisfaction that she would no longer be one of them.

He made a low, scoffing sound. "Don't be dramatic."

Dru forced herself to smile at the man who had dominated every aspect of her life, waking and sleeping and everything in between, for the past five years. Night and day. Across all time zones and into every little corner of the globe where his vast empire extended. She'd been at his beck and call around the clock as his personal assistant, dealing with anything and everything he needed dealt with, from a variety of his personal needs to the vagaries of his wide-ranging business concerns.

And she hated him. Oh, how she hated him. *She did.*

It surged in her, thick and hot and black and deep, making her skin seem to shimmer over her bones with the force of it. It was hard to imagine, now, knowing the truth, that she'd harbored softer feelings for this man for so long—but it didn't matter, she told herself sternly. It was all gone now. *Of course it was.* He'd seen to that, hadn't he?

She felt a fierce rush of that hard sort of grief that had flooded her at the strangest times in these odd few months since her twin brother Dominic had died. Life, she had come to understand all too keenly, was intense and often far too complicated to bear, but she'd soldiered on anyway. What choice was there? She'd been the only one left to handle Dominic's disease—his addictions. His care. His mountain of medical bills, the last of which she'd finally paid in full this week. And she'd been the only one left to sort through the complexities of his death, his cremation, his sad end. *That* had been hard. It still was.

But this? This was simple. This was the end of her treating herself as the person who mattered least in her life. Dru was doing her best to ignore the swirling sense of humiliation that went along with what she'd discovered in the files this morning. She assured herself that she would have resigned anyway, eventually, *soon*—that finding out what Cayo had done was only a secondary reason to leave his employ.

"This is my notice," she said calmly, in that serene and unflappable professional voice that was second nature to her—and that she resolved she would never again utilize the moment she stepped out of this office building and walked away from this man. She would cast aside the necessarily icy exterior that had seen her through these years, that had protected her from herself as well as from him. She would be as chaotic and emotional and yes, *dramatic* as she wished, whenever she wished. She would be *flappable* unto her very bones. She could already feel that shell she'd wrapped around her for so long begin to crack. "Effective immediately."

Slowly, incredulously, a kind of menace and that disconcerting pulse of power that was uniquely his emanating from him like a new kind of electricity, Cayo Vila, much-celebrated founder and CEO of the Vila Group and its impressive collection of hotels, airlines, businesses and whatever else took his fancy, richer than all manner of sins and a hundred times as ruthless, raised his head.

Dru caught her breath. His jet-black brows were low over the dark gold heat of his eyes. That fierce, uncompromising face made almost brutally sensual by his remarkable mouth that any number of pneumatic celebutantes swooned over daily was drawn into a thunderous expression that boded only ill. The shock of his full attention, the hit of it, that all these years of proximity had failed to temper or dissipate, ricocheted through her, as always.

She hated that most of all. Her damnable weakness.

The air seemed to sizzle, making the vast expanse of his office, all cold contemporary lines and sweeping glass that seemed to invite the English weather inside, seem small and tight around her.

"I beg your pardon?"

She could hear the lilt of Spanish flavor behind his words, hinting at his past and betraying the volatile temper he usually kept under tight control. Dru restrained a small ripple of sensation, very near a shiver, that snaked along her spine. They called him the Spanish Satan for a reason. *She* would like to call him far worse.

"You heard me." The bravado felt good. Almost cleansing.

He shook his head, dismissing her. "I don't have time for this," he said. "Whatever this is. Send me an email outlining your concerns and—"

"You do," she interrupted him. They both paused; perhaps both noting the fact that she had never dared interrupt him before. She smiled coolly at him as if she were unaware of his amazement at her temerity. "You do have time," she assured him. "I cleared this quarter-hour on your schedule especially."

A very tense moment passed much too slowly between them then, and he did not appear to so much as blink. And she felt the force of that attention, as if his gaze were a gas fire, burning hot and wild and charring her where she stood.

"Is this your version of a negotiation, Miss Bennett?" His tone was as cool as hers, his midnight amber gaze far hotter. "Have I neglected your performance review this year? Have you taken it upon yourself to demand more money? Better benefits?"

His voice was curt, clipped. That edge of sardonic displeasure with something darker, smokier, beneath. Behind her professional armor, Dru felt something catch. As if he could sense it, he smiled.

"This is not a negotiation and I do not want a raise or anything else," she said, matter-of-factly, wishing that after all this time, and what she now knew he'd done, she was immune to him and the wild pounding of her heart that particular smile elicited. "I don't even want a reference. This conversation is merely a courtesy."

"If you imagine that you will be taking my secrets

to any one of my competitors," he said in a casual, conversational tone that Dru knew him far too well to believe, "you should understand that if you try, I will dedicate my life to destroying you. In and out of the courts. Believe this, if nothing else."

"I love nothing more than a good threat," she replied in the same tone, though she doubted very much that it made *his* stomach knot in reaction. "But it's quite unnecessary. I have no interest in the corporate world."

His mouth moved into something too cynical to be another smile.

"Name your price, Miss Bennett," he suggested, his voice like smoke and sin, and it was no wonder at all that so many hapless rivals went over all wide-eyed and entranced and gave him whatever it was he wanted almost the very moment he demanded it. He was like some kind of corporate snake charmer.

But she wasn't one of his snakes, and she refused to dance to his tune, no matter how seductive. She'd been dancing for far too long, and this was where it ended. It had to. It would.

"I have no price," she said with perfect honesty. Once—yesterday—he could have smiled at her and she'd have found a way to storm heaven for him. But that was yesterday. Today she could only marvel, if that was the word, at how naive and gullible she'd been. At how well he'd played her.

"Everyone has a price." And in his world, she knew, this was always true. Always. One more reason she wanted to escape it. Him.

"I'm sorry, Mr. Vila," she said. She even shrugged. "I don't."

Not anymore. Dominic was gone. She was no longer his sole support. And the invisible chains of emotion and longing that had ruled her for so long could no longer keep her here. Not now she'd discovered, entirely by accident, what Cayo truly thought of her.

He only watched her now, those dark amber eyes moving over her like the touch of his hands, all fire and demand. She knew what he saw. She had crafted her corporate image specifically to appeal to his particular tastes, to acquiesce, as ever, to his preferences. She stood tall before his scrutiny, resisting the urge to fuss with her pencil skirt or the silk blouse she wore, both in the muted colors he preferred. She knew the deceptively simple twist that held her dark brown hair up was elegant, perfect. There was no bold jewelry that he might find "distracting." Her cosmetics were carefully applied, as always, to keep her looking fresh and neat and as if she hardly needed any at all, as if she simply possessed a perfect skin tone, attractively shaded lips and bright eyes without effort. She had become so good at playing this role, at being precisely what he wanted. She'd done it for so long. She could do it in her sleep. She had.

Dru could see the precise moment he realized that she was serious, that this wasn't merely a bargaining tactic she was trotting out as some kind of strategic attempt to get something from him. That she meant what she was saying, however impossible he found it to fathom. The impatience faded from his clever gaze and turned to something far more calculating—almost brooding. He lounged back against his massive, deliberately intimidating chair, propped his jaw on his hand, and treated her to the full force of that brilliant, impossible focus of his that made him such a devastating opponent. *No* was never a final answer, not to Cayo Vila. It was where he began. Where he came alive.

And where she got off, this time. For good. She couldn't help the little flare of satisfaction she got from knowing that she would be the one thing he couldn't *mogul* his way into winning. Not anymore. Not ever again.

"What is this?" he asked quietly, sounding perfectly reasonable, having obviously concluded that he could manipulate her better with a show of interest in what she might be feeling than the sort of offensive strategy he might otherwise employ. "Are you unhappy?"

What a preposterous question. Dru let out a short laugh that clearly hit him the wrong way. In truth, she'd known it would. His eyes narrowed, seeming almost to glow with the temper that would show only there, she was well aware. He so rarely unleashed the full force of it. It normally only lurked, beneath everything, like a dark promise no one wanted him to keep.

"Of course I'm unhappy," she replied, keeping herself from rolling her eyes by the barest remaining shred of her once iron control. "I have no personal life. I have no life at all, in point of fact, and haven't for five years. I manage yours instead."

"For which you are extraordinarily well paid," he pointed out. With bite.

"I know you won't believe me," she said, almost pityingly, which made his eyes narrow even further, "and you will certainly never discover this on your own, God knows, but there is more to life than money."

Again, that shrewd amber stare.

"Is this about a man?" he asked in a voice she might have called something like disgruntled had it belonged to someone else. She laughed again, and told herself she couldn't hear the edge in it, that he should hit so

close to a bitter truth she had no intention of acknowl-
edging.

"When do you imagine I would have the time to
meet men?" she asked. "In between assignments and
business trips? While busy sending farewell gifts to
all of *your* ex-lovers?"

"Ah," he said, in a tone that put her back right up, so
condescending was it. "I understand now." His smile
then was both patronizing and razor-sharp. Dru felt
it drag across her, clawing deep. "I suggest you take
a week's holiday, Miss Bennett. Perhaps two. Find a
beach and some warm bodies. Drink something potent
and scratch the itch. As many times as necessary. You
are of no use to me at all in this state."

"That is a charming idea," Dru said, something dark
and destructive churning inside her, through lips that
felt pale with rage, "and I appreciate the offer, naturally.
But I am not you, Mr. Vila." She let everything she felt
about him—all these years of longing and sacrifice,
all the things she'd thought and hoped, all the foolish
dreams she'd had no idea he'd crushed in their infancy
until today, even that one complicated and emotional
night in Cadiz three years ago they never discussed
and never would—burn through her as she stared at
him. "I do not 'scratch the itch' with indiscriminate
abandon, leaving masses in my wake, like some kind
of oversexed Godzilla. I have standards."

He blinked. He did not move a single other muscle
and yet Dru had to order herself to stay in place, so
powerfully did she *feel* the lash of his temper, the kick
of those amber eyes as they bored into her.

"Are you unwell?" he asked with soft menace, only
the granite set of his jaw and the deepening of his accent hinting at his mounting fury. But Dru knew him.

She knew the danger signs when she saw them. "Or have you taken complete leave of your senses?"

"This is called *honesty,* Mr. Vila," she replied with a crispness that completely belied the alarms ringing wildly inside her, screaming at her to run, to leave at once, to stop *taunting* him, for God's sake, as if that would prod him into being who she'd imagined he was! "I understand that it's not something you're familiar with, particularly not from me. But that's what happens when one is as carelessly domineering and impossible as you pride yourself on being. You are surrounded by an obsequious echo chamber of minions and acolytes, too afraid of you to speak the truth. I should know. I've been pretending to be one among them for years."

He went terrifyingly still. She could feel his temper expand to fill the room, all but rattling the windows. She could see that lean, muscled body of his seem to hum with the effort she imagined it took him to keep from exploding along with it. His gaze locked on hers, dark and furious. Infinitely more lethal than she wanted to admit to herself.

Or maybe it was that she was simply too susceptible to him. Still. *Always,* something inside her whispered, making her despair of herself anew.

"I suggest you think very carefully about the next thing that comes out of your mouth," he said in that deceptively measured way, the cruelty he was famous for rich in his voice then, casting his fierce face into iron. "You may otherwise live to regret it."

This time, Dru's laugh was real. If, she could admit to herself, a little bit nervous.

"That's what you don't understand," she said, grief and satisfaction and too many other things stamping through her, making her feel wild and dangerously close to a certain kind of fierce, possibly unhinged joy. That she was defying him? That she was actually getting to him, for once? She had no idea anymore. "I don't care. I'm essentially bulletproof. What are you going to do? Sack me? Blacklist me? Refuse me a reference? Go right ahead. I've already quit."

And then, at long last, fulfilling the dream she'd cherished in one form or another since she'd taken this horribly all-consuming job in the first place purely to pay for Dominic's assorted bills—because she couldn't help but love her brother, despite everything and because she was all he'd had, and that had meant something to her even when she'd wished it didn't—Dru turned her back on Cayo Vila, her own personal demon and the greatest bane of her existence, and walked out of his life forever.

Just as she'd originally planned she would someday.

There really should have been trumpets, at the very least. And certainly no trace of that hard sort of anguish that swam in her and made this much, much more difficult than it should have been.

She was almost to the far door of the outer office, where her desk sat as guardian of this most inner sanctum, when he snapped out her name. It was a stark command, and she had been too well trained to ignore it. She stopped, hating herself for obeying him, but it was only this last time, she told herself. What could it hurt?

When she looked over her shoulder, she felt a chill of surprise that he was so close behind her without her having heard him move, but she couldn't think about that—it was that look on his face that struck her, all thunder and warning, and her heart began to pound, hard.

"If memory serves," he said in a cool tone that was at complete odds with that dark savagery in his burnished gold gaze, "your contract states that you must give me two weeks following the tendering of your notice."

It was Dru's turn to blink. "You're not serious."

"I may be an 'oversexed Godzilla,' Miss Bennett..." He bit out each word like a bullet she shouldn't have been able to feel, and yet it hurt—it *hurt*—and all the while the gold in his gaze seemed to sear into her, making her remember all the things she'd rather forget. "But that has yet to impede my ability to read a contract. Two weeks, which, if I am not mistaken, includes the investor dinner in Milan we've spent months planning."

"Why would you want that?" Dru found she'd turned to face him without meaning to move, and her hands had become fists at her sides. "Are you that perverse?"

"I'm surprised you haven't already found the answer to that from my ex-lovers, with whom you are so close, apparently," he threw at her, his voice a sardonic lash. "Didn't you spend all of those hours of your wasted life placating them?"

He folded his arms over his chest, and Dru found herself noticing, as always, the sheer, lean perfection of his athletic form. It was part of what made him so deadly. So dizzyingly unmanageable. Every inch of him was a finely honed weapon, and he was not averse to using whatever part of that weapon would best serve him. That was why, she understood, he was standing over her like this, intimidating her with the fact of his height, the breadth of his shoulders, the inexorable force and power of his relentless masculinity. Even in a bespoke suit which should have made him look like some kind of dandy, he looked capable of anything. There was that hint of wildness about him, that constant, underlying *threat* he wore proudly. Deliberately.

She didn't want to see him as a man. She didn't want to remember the heat of his hands against her skin, his mouth so demanding on hers. She would die before she gave him the satisfaction of seeing that he got to her now. Even if she still felt the burn of it, the searing fire.

"You know what they say," she murmured, sounding almost entirely calm to her own ears. Almost blasé. "Those who sleep with someone for the money earn every penny."

He didn't appear to react to that at all, and yet she felt something hard and hot flare between them, almost making her step back, almost making her show him exactly how nervous he made her. But she was done with that. With him. She refused to cower before him. And she was finished with quiet obedience, too. Look what it had got her.

"Take the rest of the day off," he suggested then, a certain hoarseness in his voice the only hint of the fury she couldn't quite see but had no doubt was close to liquefying them both. And perhaps the whole of the office building they stood in as well, if not the entire City of London besides. "I suggest you do something to curb your newfound urge toward candid commentary. I'll see you tomorrow morning. Half-seven, as usual, Miss Bennett."

And it was suddenly as if a new sun dawned, bathing Dru in a bright, impossible light. Everything became stark and clear. He loomed there, not three feet away from her, taking up too much space, dark and impossible and faintly terrifying even when quiet and watchful. And he would never stop. She understood that about him; she understood it the way she comprehended her own ability to breathe. His entire life was a testament to his inability to take no for an answer, to not accept what others told him if it wasn't something he wanted to hear. He had never encountered a rule he didn't break, a wall he couldn't climb, a barrier he wouldn't slap down simply because it dared to stand in his way.

He *took*. That was what he did. At the most basic level, that was who Cayo Vila was.

He'd taken from her and she hadn't even known it until today, had she? Some part of her—even now—wished she'd never opened that file drawer, never discovered how easily he'd derailed her career three years ago without her ever the wiser. But she had.

She could see the whole rest of her life flash before her eyes in a sickening, infinitely depressing cascade of images. If she agreed to his two weeks, she might as well die on the spot. Right here, right now. Because he would take possession of her life the way he'd done of her last five years, and there would be no end to it. Ever. Dru knew perfectly well that she was the best personal assistant he'd ever had. That wasn't any immodesty on her part—she'd had to be, because she'd needed the money he'd paid her and the cachet his name had afforded her when it came time to wrangle Dominic into the best drug-treatment clinics and programs in the States, for all the good it had done. And she still believed it had all been worth it, no matter how little she had to show for it now, no matter how empty and battered she felt. Dominic had not died alone, on a lonely street corner in some desperate city neighborhood, never to be identified or mourned or missed. That was what mattered.

But Dominic had only been the first, original reason. Her pathetic feelings for Cayo had been the second—and far more appalling—reason she'd made herself so indispensible to Cayo. She'd taken pride in her ability to serve him so well. It left a bitter taste in her mouth today, but it was true. She was that much of a masochist, and she'd have to live with that. If she stayed even one day more, any chance she had left to reclaim her life, to do something for herself, to *live,* to crawl out of this terrible hole she'd lowered herself into all on her own, would disappear into the big black smoke-filled vortex that was Cayo Vila.

He would buy more things and sell others, make millions and destroy lives at a whim, hers included. And she would carry on catering to him, jumping to do his bidding and smoothing the path before him, anticipating his every need and losing herself, bit by bit and inch by inch, until she was nothing more than a pleasant-looking, serene-voiced husk. A robot under his command. Slave to feelings he would never, could never return, despite small glimmers to the contrary in far-off cities on complicated evenings never spoken of aloud when they were done.

Worse, she would *want* to do all of it. She would *want* to be whatever she could be for him, just so long as she could stay near him. Just as she had since that night she'd seen such a different side of him in Cadiz. She would cling to anything, wouldn't she? She would even pretend she didn't know that he'd crushed her dreams of advancement with a single, brutal email. She was, she knew, exactly that pathetic. Exactly that stupid. Hadn't she proved it every single day of these past three years?

"No," she said.

It was, of course, a word he rarely heard.

His black brows lowered. His hard gold eyes shone with amazement. That impossibly lush mouth, the one that made his parade of lovers fantasize that there could be some softness to him, only to discover too late that it was no more than a mirage, flattened ominously.

"What do you mean, no?"

The lilt of his native Spanish cadence made the words sound almost musical, but Dru knew that the thicker his accent, the more trouble she was in—and the closer that volcanic temper of his was to eruption. She should have turned on her heel and run for safety. She should have heeded the knot in her belly and the heat that moved over her skin, the panic that flooded through her.

"I understand that you might not be familiar with the word," she said, sounding perhaps more empowered, more sure of herself, than was wise. Or true. "It indicates dissent. Refusal. Both concepts you have difficulty with, I know. But that is, I am happy to say, no longer my problem."

"It will become your problem," he told her, a note she'd never heard before in his voice. His gaze narrowed further, into two outraged slits of gold, as if he'd never actually seen her until this moment. Something about that particular way he looked at her made her feel lightheaded. "I will—"

"Go ahead and take me to court," she said, interrupting him again with a careless wave of her hand that, she could see, visibly infuriated him. "What do you think you'll win?"

For the first time in as long as she'd known him, Cayo Vila was rendered speechless. The silence was taut and breathless between them, and, still, was some-

how as loud as a siren. It seemed to *hum*. And he simply stared at her, thunderstruck, an expression she had
never seen before on his ruthless face.

Good.

"Will you take my flat from me?" she continued,
warming to the topic. Emboldened, perhaps, by his un-
precedented silence. By the chaos inside of her that was
all his fault. "It's only a leased bedsit. You're welcome
to it. I'll write you a check right now, if you like, for
the entire contents of my current account. Is that what
it will take?" She laughed, and could hear it bouncing
back at her from the glass wall, the tidy expanse of her
desk, even the polished floor that made even the outer
office seem glossy and that much more intimidating
to the unwary. "I've already given you five years. I'm
not giving you two more weeks. I'm not giving you
another second. I'd rather die."

Cayo stared at his assistant as if he'd never seen her
before.

There was something about the way she tilted that
perfect, pretty oval of her face, the way her usually
calm gray eyes sparkled with the force of her temper,
and something about that mouth of hers. He couldn't
seem to look away from it.

Unbidden, a memory teased through his head, of her
hand on his cheek, her gray eyes warm and something
like affectionate, her lips—but no. There was no need
to revisit *that* insanity. He'd worked much too hard
to strike it from his consciousness. It was one regret-
table evening in five smooth, issue-free years. Why
think of it at all?

"I would rather die," she said again, as if she was

under the misapprehension that he had not heard her the first time.

"That can always be arranged," he said, searching that face he knew so well and yet, apparently, so little—looking for some clue as to what had brought this on. Here, now, today. "Have you forgotten? I am a very formidable man."

"If you are going to make threats, Mr. Vila," she replied in that crisp way of hers, "at least pay me the compliment of making them credible. You are many things, but you are not a thug. As such."

For the first time in longer than he could remember—since, perhaps, he had been the fatherless child whose mother, all the village had known too well, had been so disgraced that she had taken to the convent after his birth rather than face the wages of her sin in its ever-growing flesh—Cayo was at a loss. It might have amused him that it was his personal assistant who had wrought this level of incapacity in him, his glorified secretary for God's sake, when nothing else had managed it. Not another multimillion-pound deal, not one more scandalous affair reported breathlessly and inaccurately in the tabloids, not one of his new and—dare he say it—visionary business enterprises. Nothing got beneath his skin. Nothing threw him off balance.

Only this woman. As she had once before.

It was funny. It was. He was certain he would laugh about it at some point, and at great length, but first? He needed her. Back in line where she belonged, back securely in the role he preferred her to play, and he ignored the small whisper inside him that suggested that there would be no repairing this. That she would never again be as comfortably invisible as she'd been before, that it was too late, that he'd been operating on borrowed time since the incident in Cadiz three years ago and this was only the delayed fallout—

"I am leaving," she told him, meeting his gaze as if he were a naughty child in the midst of a tiresome strop, and enunciating each word as if she suspected he was too busy tantruming to hear her otherwise. "You will have to come to terms with that and if you feel it necessary to file suit against me, have at it. I booked a ticket to Bora Bora this morning. I'm sorted."

And then, finally, his brain started working again. It was one thing for her to take herself off to wherever she lived in London, or even off on a week's holiday to, say, Ibiza, as he'd suggested. But French Polynesia, a world away? Unacceptable.

Because he could not let her go. He refused. And he wanted to examine that as little as he had the last time he'd discovered that she wanted to leave him. Three years ago, only a week after that night in Cadiz he'd seen—and still saw—no point in dredging forth.

It wasn't personal, of course, then or now; she was an asset. In many ways, the most valuable asset he had. She knew too much about him. Everything, in fact, from his inseam to his favorite breakfast to his preferred concierge service in all the major cities around the globe, to say nothing of the ins and outs of the way he handled his business affairs. He couldn't imagine how long it would take to train up her replacement, and he had no intention of finding out. He would do as he always did—whatever was necessary to protect his assets. Whatever it took.

"I apologize for my behavior," he said then, almost formally. He shifted his stance and thrust his hands into the pockets of his trousers, rocking back on his heels in a manner he knew was the very opposite of aggressive. "You took me by surprise." Her gray eyes narrowed suspiciously, and he wished that he had taken the time to learn how to read her as thoroughly as he knew she could read him. It put him at a disadvantage, another unfamiliar sensation.

"Of course I will not sue you," he continued, forcing himself to keep an even, civil tone, and the rest of himself in check. "I was simply reacting badly, as anyone would. You are the best personal assistant I've ever had. Perhaps the best in all of London. I am quite sure you know this."

"Well," she said, dropping her gaze, which he found unaccountably fascinating. She said something almost under her breath then, something that sounded very much like *that's nothing to be proud of, is it?*

Cayo wanted to pursue that, but didn't. He had every intention of cracking her wide open and figuring out every last one of her mysteries until he was sure that none remained, that she could never take him by surprise again, but not now. Not here. Not until he'd dealt with this situation the only way he knew how.

Which was to dominate it and contain it and make it his, by whatever means necessary.

"As you must be aware, however," he continued, "there will be a great number of papers to sign before you can leave the company. Confidentiality agreements being the least of it." He checked the watch on his wrist with a quick snap of his arm. "It's still early. We can leave immediately."

"Leave?" she echoed, openly frowning now, which was when it occurred to him that he'd never seen her do that before—she was always so very serene, with only the odd flash in her eyes to hint at what went on in her head. He'd never wanted to know. But this was a full frown, brows drawn and that mouth of hers tight, and he was riveted. Why could he not tear his attention away from her mouth? The lines he'd never seen before, making the smooth expanse of her forehead more interesting somehow? It made him much too close to uncomfortable. As if she was a real person instead of merely his most prized possession, exhibiting brand-new traits. Worse, as if she was a woman.

But he didn't want to think about that. He certainly didn't want to remember the only other time he'd seen her as anything more than his assistant. He didn't want this woman in his bed. Of course he didn't. She was too clever, too good at what she did. He wanted her at his beck and call, at his side, where she belonged.

"My entire legal team is in Zurich," he reminded her gently. "Surely you have not forgotten that already in your haste to leave?"

He watched her stiffen, and thought she would balk at the idea of a quick trip to Switzerland, but instead, she swallowed. Visibly. And then squared her shoulders as if a not-quite-two-hour trip on the private jet was akin to a trial by fire. One that she was reluctantly willing to suffer through, if it would rid her of him.

"Fine," she said, with an impatient sort of sigh that he did not care for in the least. "If you want me to sign something, anything, I'll sign it. Even in bloody Zurich, if you insist. I want this over with."

And Cayo smiled, because he had her.

CHAPTER TWO

By the time the helicopter touched down on the helipad on the foredeck of the gently moving luxury yacht, Dru had worked herself into what she could only call a state.

She climbed out of the sleek little machine only when she realized she had no other choice, that the pilot was shutting it down and preparing to stay on board the great yacht himself—and Dru did not fancy spending who knew how long sitting in a helicopter simply to prove a point. She was quite certain that Cayo would leave her there.

On some level, she was bitterly aware she really should have expected he'd pull a stunt like this. Unabashed abduction. Simply because he could.

So, in spite of the fact that she wanted to put whole worlds between them, she found herself following Cayo's determined, athletic stride across the deck, too upset to really take in the sparkling blue sea on all sides and what she was afraid was the Croatian mainland in the distance. The sea air teased tendrils of her hair out of the twist that had been carefully calibrated to withstand the London drizzle, and she actually had a familiar moment of panic, out of habit, as if it should still matter to her what she looked like. As if she should still be concerned that he might find her professional appearance wanting in some way. It appalled her how deep it went in her, this knee-jerk need to please him. It was going to take her a whole lot longer to quit the Cayo Vila habit than she'd like.

And the fact that he had spirited her away to the wrong country didn't help.

"You do realize this is kidnapping, don't you?" she demanded. Not for the first time. The difference was that this time, Cayo actually stopped and looked at her, turning his dark head slowly so that his hard gaze made every hair on her body prickle to attention. She sucked in a breath.

"What on earth are you talking about?" he asked silkily. At his most dangerous, but she couldn't let that intimidate her. She wouldn't. "Nobody forced you to come on this trip. There was no gun to your back. You agreed."

"This is not Switzerland," she pointed out, trying to keep her rising panic at bay. "It doesn't even resemble Switzerland. The sea is a dead giveaway and unless I am very much mistaken, that is Dubrovnik."

She stabbed a finger in the general direction of the red-roofed, whitewashed city that clung to the rugged coastline off the side of the yacht, and the walls and fortress that encircled it so protectively. The blue waters of the Adriatic—because she knew where she was, she didn't need him to confirm it so much as explain it—were as gorgeous and inviting as ever. She wanted to throw him overboard and watch those same waters consume him, inch by aggravating inch. Only the fact that he was so much bigger than she—and all of it sleek and smooth muscle she did not trust herself near enough to touch—prevented her trying. And only barely prevented her, at that.

He didn't glance toward the shore. Why should he? He had undoubtedly known where they were going the moment he'd mentioned Zurich back in London. He'd certainly known when they'd landed in a mysterious airfield somewhere in Europe and he'd hurried her onto the helicopter before she could get her bearings. This was only a surprise for *her.*

"Did I say Switzerland?" he asked, that voice of his deceptively soft and all the more lethal for it, while his gaze remained hard. "You must have misheard me."

"Exactly what is your plan?' she threw at him, temper and fear and something else she couldn't quite identify sloshing around inside her, making her feel like a bomb about to detonate. "Am I your prisoner now?"

"How theatrical you are," he said, and she had the impression that he was choosing his words carefully. That much harsher words lurked behind that quiet tone that she knew meant he was furious. "How did you manage to hide that so long and so well?"

"You must have mistaken me for someone else," Dru hurled at him. "I'm not going to mindlessly obey your commands—"

"Are you certain?" That black gold gaze of his turned darker, harder as he cut her off. It made her feel oddly hollow, and much too hot. She assured herself it was anger, nothing more. "If memory serves, obedience is one of your strengths."

"Obedience was my job," she said with some remnant of her former iciness. "But I quit."

He looked at her for a long, simmering moment.

"Your resignation has not been accepted, Miss Bennett," he snapped out, fierce and commanding. As if she should not dare mention the matter again. And then he turned his back on her and strode off across the gleaming, sun-kissed deck as if it was settled.

Dru stood where he'd left her, feeling a little bit silly and more than a little off balance in her smart office clothes and delicate heels that were completely inappropriate for a boat. She stepped out of her stilettos and scooped them up in her hand, trying to breathe in the crisp sea air. Trying to curl her now-bare toes against the cool deck as if that might ground her.

Trying to breathe.

She moved over to the polished rail and leaned her elbows against it, frowning at the rolling waves, the gorgeously craggy coastline beckoning in the distance, rich dark greens and weathered reds basking in the sun. She felt it all twist and shift inside her then, all of the struggle and agony, the sacrifice and frustrated yearning. The grief. The hope. The brutal truth some part of her wished she'd never learned. It all seemed to swell within her as if it might crack her open and rip her apart—as if, having finally opened the door to all the things she'd repressed all this time, the lies she'd told herself, she couldn't lock it back up. She couldn't pretend any longer.

Misery rose inside her, thick and black and suffocating. And fast. And for a moment, she could do nothing but let it claim her. There was so much she couldn't change, couldn't help. She couldn't go back in time and keep her father from dying when she and Dominic had still been toddlers. She couldn't keep her mother from her string of lovers, each more vicious and abusive than the last. She couldn't keep sweet, sensitive Dominic from choosing oblivion, and then courting it, his life and his drugs getting harder every year, until it was no more than a waiting game for his inevitable and tragic end.

The long, hard breath she took felt ragged. Too close to painful.

And she was free of those obligations now, it was true, but she was also irrevocably and impossibly alone. She hardly remembered her father and her mother hadn't acknowledged her existence in years. She'd built her life around handling Dominic's disease, and with him gone, there was nothing but…emptiness. She would fill it, she promised herself. She would build a life based finally on what she wanted, not as some kind of response to people and things that were forever out of her control. Not a life in opposition to her mother's choices. Not a life contingent on Dominic's problems. A life that was only hers, whatever that looked like.

All she had to do was escape Cayo Vila first.

Another fresh wave of pain crashed through her then, just as hard to fight off. Sharper, somehow. Wrenching and dark. *Cayo.* Three years ago she'd thought she'd seen something in him, some glimmer of humanity, an indication that he was so much more than the man he pretended to be in public. And she'd taken that night, some intimate conversation and a single, ill-conceived, far too passionate kiss, and built herself a whole imaginary world of possibility. Oh, the ways she'd wanted him, the ways she'd believed in him—and all the while he'd thought so very little of her that he'd blocked her chances for another position in the Vila Group and, in so doing, any kind of independent career. Without a word to her. Without any conversation at all.

With three careless sentences.

Miss Bennett is an assistant, he'd emailed Human

Resources not long after that night she'd so foolishly believed had changed everything between them. She'd applied for the job in marketing, thinking it was high time she spread her wings in the company, took charge of her own career rather than merely supported his. *She is certainly no vice president. Look elsewhere.*

He hadn't hidden the fact he'd done it, either. Why should he have? It was right there in Dru's file, had she ever bothered to look. She hadn't, until today, while doing a bit of housecleaning about the office. She'd been so sure everything was different after Cadiz, if unspoken, unaddressed. She hadn't minded that she hadn't got that job; she'd thought she and Cayo had an understanding—she'd believed they were a team—

So help her, she thought now, forcing back the angry, humiliated tears she was determined not to cry, she would never again be so foolish.

She'd known exactly who he was when he'd hired her, and she knew exactly who he was now. She'd spend the rest of her life working out how she'd managed to lose sight of that for so long, how she'd betrayed herself so completely for a fantasy life in her head, built around a single kiss that still made her flush hot to recall, but she wouldn't forget herself again. It was cold comfort, perhaps, but it was all she had.

She found him in one of the yacht's many salons, a sleek celebration of marble and glass down an ostentatious spiral stair that was as gloriously luxe as everything else on this floating castle he'd won in a late-night card game from a Russian oligarch.

"It was easy to take," he'd said with a small shrug when she'd asked why he'd wanted another yacht to add to his collection. "So I took it."

He sat now in the sunken seating area with one of

his interchangeable and well-nigh-anonymous compan-
ions melting all over him, all plumped-up breasts and
sheaves of wheat-blond hair cascading here and there.
He had discarded his jacket somewhere and now looked
deliciously rumpled, white shirt open at the collar and
his olive skin seeming to gleam. The girl pouted and
whined something in what sounded like Czech when
she saw Dru walk in, as if it was Dru's presence that
was keeping Cayo's attention on the flat-screen television on the inner wall rather than on the assets she had
on display. As if, were Dru not there, he might actually
pay her some mind.

You are fast approaching your expiration date,
Dru seethed uncharitably at the other woman, but then
caught herself. This was not a cat fight. It wasn't even
a competition.

Dru had spent entirely too long telling herself that
it was all perfectly fine with her, that she didn't mind
at all that this man who had kissed her with so much
heat and longing in an ancient city, and who had looked
at her as if she were the only person in the world who
could ever matter to him, slaked his various lusts with
all of these anonymous women. *Why should it matter?* she'd argued with herself a thousand times in the
middle of the night while she lay alone and he was off
tending to his companion du jour. *What we have is so
much deeper than sex...*

It was all so desperate. So delusional and terribly,
gut-wrenchingly pathetic.

She held a shoe in each hand now, like potential
weapons, and she allowed herself a grim moment of
amusement as she watched Cayo's ever-calculating
gaze move to the sharp stiletto heels immediately, as
if he joined her in imagining her sinking them deep

into his jugular. He smirked and returned his attention to the television and the almighty scroll of the New York Stock Exchange across the bottom of the screen, as if he'd assessed the threat that quickly and dismissed it that easily.

And her. Again. As ever.

"Have you finished having your little fit?" he asked. She felt her heart race, that same anger—at him and, worse, at herself—shaking through her, making her very nearly tremble.

"I want to know what you think is going to happen now that you've stranded me on this boat," Dru replied, biting the words out. "Will you simply keep me imprisoned here forever? That seems impractical, at the very least. Boats eventually dock, and I can swim."

"I suggest you take a deep breath, Miss Bennett," he said in that obnoxiously patronizing tone, not even bothering to glance at her again, his entire lean body insulting in its disinterest. "You are becoming hysterical."

It was too much, finally. She didn't even think.

She cocked one arm back in a moment of searing, possibly insane, mind-numbing rage and threw a shoe.

At his head.

It sliced through the air, the wicked heel seeming almost to glow, and she pictured it spearing him directly between the mocking, impossible eyes—

But then he reached up and snatched it out of its flight at the last moment, his hand too large and masculine against the delicate point of the heel.

When he looked at her then, his dark golden stare burned with outrage. And something else—something that seemed to echo in her, hard and loud. Anticipation? The shared memory of an old street, that explosive kiss? But no, that was impossible. Nothing more than her desperate fantasies in action yet again.

Dru panted slightly, as if that had been her in vicious flight. As if he now held her like that, captured against his hard palm. That same current of wild, hot heat that she wished was simple fury seemed to coil within her and then pulse low, the way it always did when he was near.

"Next time," she told him from between her teeth, her other hand clenching her remaining shoe, heel first, "I won't miss."

Once again, she'd surprised him. And he liked it as little as he had in London.

Her gray gaze was alert and intent and he didn't like all the things he could see in it, none of which he understood or wanted to try to understand. He didn't like the faint flush on her cheeks, or the way she looked with her feet bare and her hair something other than perfect for the first time in as long as he'd known her. *Sexy.*

He had to jerk his gaze from hers and when he did, he found himself looking down at the vicious little stiletto she'd flung at his throat. It was a weapon, certainly, but it was also one of those delicate, wickedly feminine shoes that he did not want to think about in reference to his personal assistant. He did not want to imagine her slipping the sleek little shoe on over those elegant feet of hers that he'd never noticed before, or think about what the saucy height of the heel would do to her hips as she walked—

Damn her.

Cayo rose to his feet slowly, not taking his eyes from hers.

"What am I going to do with you?" he asked, impatient with her defiance. And equally impatient with his own failure to end this distracting and disruptive situation that was already well out of hand. But those errant strands of silky dark hair teased at the curve of her lips, her chin, and he could not seem to look away.

"You have had a number of options of things to do with me over the years," she pointed out, in something less than her usual crisp tone. As if she was boiling over with fury, which he should not find as compelling as he did. "You could have let me move to a different position in your company, for example. You could have let me go today. You opted to kidnap me instead."

Abruptly, Cayo remembered that they were not alone. He dismissed the clingy blonde with a careless wave of his hand and ignored the sulky expression that followed it. The woman huffed and muttered as she exited the salon, irritating him far more than she should have. Could not one female in his usually carefully controlled existence do as he wished today? Must everything be a trial?

He tossed Drusilla's stiletto down on the seat where the blonde had been, and wondered why he was even having this conversation in the first place. Why was he encouraging Drusilla further by allowing her to speak to him in that decidedly disrespectful tone?

And why on earth did he have the wholly uncharacteristic urge to explain the reasons he'd shot down her bid for that promotion three years ago? What was the matter with him? The last time he'd defended or justified his behavior was...never.

"I don't share my things," he said then, coolly, purely to put her in her place. She stiffened, and then what could only be hurt washed through her gray eyes. And for the first time in years, Cayo felt the faintest hint of something that might have been shame move through him. He ignored it.

"I'd ask you what kind of man you are to say something so deliberately insulting and borderline sociopathic, but please." Drusilla sniffed, her eyes still wounded, which he hated more than he should have. "We both already know exactly what kind of man you are, don't we?"

"The papers call me a force of nature," he replied, his voice light if cold, and it was a reminder. The last one he planned to give her. He was not a man who suffered insubordination, and yet he'd been tolerating hers for hours, up to and including an attempted attack on his person. Had she been a man, he would have responded in kind.

Basta ya! he thought, impatiently. Enough was enough.

He found himself moving toward her, tracking the nervous swallow she took as he came closer, as if she was neither as disgusted nor as impassive as she appeared. That same, seductive memory rolled over then inside him, and shook itself awake. Dangerously awake.

She shifted her weight from one bare foot to the other, reminding him as she did so that she was, in fact, a woman. Not a perfect robot built only to serve his needs as any good assistant should. That she was made of smooth, soft flesh and that her legs were perfectly formed beneath that sleek skirt. That she was not the ice sculpture of his imagination, nor a shadow. And that he'd tasted her heat himself.

He didn't like that, either. But he let his gaze fall over her anyway, noting as if for the first time that her trim figure boasted lush curves in all the right places, had he only let himself pay closer attention to them.

Something about her disheveled hair, the temper in her gaze, the complete lack of her usual calm expression was getting under his skin. His heart began to beat in a rhythm that boded only ill, and made him think of things he knew he shouldn't. Those sleek legs wrapped around his waist as he held her against a wall in the old city. That mouth of hers hot and wet beneath his. That cool competence of hers he'd depended upon all these years, melting all around him…

Unacceptable. There was a reason he never let himself think of that night, damn it. Damn *her.*

"Calling you a force of nature rather takes away from your responsibility, doesn't it?" she asked, as if she didn't notice or care that he was bearing down on her, though he saw her fingers tighten around the shoe she still clutched in one hand. "You're not a deadly hurricane or an earthquake, Mr. Vila. You're an insulated, selfish man with too much money and too few social skills."

"I believe I preferred you the way you were before," he observed then, his voice like a blade, though she didn't flinch.

"Subservient?"

"Quiet."

Her lips crooked into something much too cold to be a smile. "If you don't wish to hear my voice or my opinions, you need only let me go," she reminded him. "You are so good at dismissing people, aren't you? Didn't I watch you do it to that poor girl not five minutes ago?"

He took advantage of his superior height and leaned over her, putting his face entirely too close to hers. He could smell the faintest hint of something sweet—soap or perfume, he couldn't tell. But desire curled through him, kicking up flames. He remembered burying his face in her neck, and the need to do it again, *now,* howled through him, shocking in its intensity. And he didn't know if he admired her or wanted to throttle her when she didn't move so much as an inch. When she showed no regard at all for her own safety. When, instead, she all but *bristled* in further defiance.

He had the strangest feeling—he wouldn't call it a premonition—that this woman might very well be the death of him. He shook it off, annoyed at himself and the kind of superstitious silliness he thought he'd left behind in his unhappy childhood.

"Why are you so concerned with the fate of 'that poor girl'?" he asked, his voice dipping lower the more furious he became. "Do you even know her name?"

"Do you?" she threw back at him, even angling closer in outraged emphasis, as if she was seconds away from poking at him with something more than her words. "I'm sure I drew up the usual nondisclosure agreement whenever and wherever you picked her up—"

"Why do you care how I treat my women, Miss Bennett?" he asked icily. Dangerously. In a tone that should have silenced her for days.

"Why don't you?" she countered, scowling at him, notably unsilenced.

And suddenly, he understood what was happening. It was all too obvious, and what concerned him was that he hadn't seen this boiling in her, as it must have done for years. He hadn't let a single meaningless night, deliberately ignored almost as soon as it had happened, haunt him or affect their working relationship. He'd thought she hadn't, either.

"Perhaps," he suggested in a tone that brooked no more of her nonsense, "when I asked you if there was a man and you denied it, you were not being entirely forthcoming, were you?"

For a moment she only stared back at him, blankly. Then she sucked in a breath as shocked, incredulous understanding flooded her gaze—followed by a sudden flare of awareness, hot and unmistakable. She jerked back. But he had already seen it.

"You are joking," she breathed. She sounded horrified. Appalled. Perhaps a bit too horrified and appalled, come to that. "You actually think… *You?*"

"Me," he agreed, all of that simmering fury shifting inside him, rolling over into something else, something he remembered all too well, despite his claims to the contrary. "You would hardly be the first secretary in history to have a bit of a sad crush on her boss, would you?" He inclined his head, feeling magnanimous. "And I will take responsibility for it, of course. I should not have let Cadiz happen. It was my fault. I allowed you to entertain…ideas."

She seemed to pale before him, and despite himself, despite what he said and what he wanted, all he could think about was that long-ago night, the Spanish air soft around him as they'd walked back to their hotel from the bodega, the world pleasantly blurry and her arm around his waist as if he'd needed help. Support. And then her mouth beneath his, her tongue, her taste, far more intoxicating than the *manzanilla* he'd drunk in some kind of twisted tribute to the grandfather whose death that same day he'd refused to mourn. He'd kissed her instead. There'd been the wall. The sweet darkness. His hands against her curves, his mouth on her neck… All these years later, he could taste her still.

He'd been lying to himself. This was not just annoyance, anger, that moved in him, making him hard and ready, making his blood race through his veins. This was *want*.

"I would be more likely to have a 'crush' on the Grim Reaper," she was saying furiously, her words tripping over each other as if she couldn't say them fast enough. "That sounds infinitely preferable, in fact, scythe and all. And I was your personal assistant, not your secretary—"

"You're whatever I say you are." His tone was silken and vicious, as if that could banish the memory, or put it where it belonged. And her and this driving *want* of her with it. "Something you seem to have forgot completely today, along with your place."

She sucked in a breath, and he saw it again—that flash of sizzling awareness, of sexual heat. Of memory. That light in her gray eyes that he'd seen once before and had not forgotten at all, much as he'd told himself he'd done. Much as he'd wanted to do.

More lies, he knew now, as his body hummed with the need to taste her. Possess her.

"I haven't wasted a single second 'entertaining ideas' about your drunken boorishness in Cadiz," she hissed at him, but her voice caught and he knew she was as much a liar as he was. "About one little kiss. Have you? Is that why you blocked me from that promotion? Some kind of jealousy?"

He wasn't jealous, of course, it was a laughable idea—but he wanted that taste of her and he wanted her quiet, and there was only one way he could think of to achieve both of those things at once. He told himself it was strategy.

His heart pounded. He wanted his hands on her. *He wanted.*

Strategy, he thought again.

And he didn't quite believe his own story, but he bent his head anyway, and kissed her.

It was as if the air between them simply burst into flame.

Or perhaps that was her.

This cannot be happening again—

But Dru had no time to think anything further. His mouth was on hers, *his beautiful mouth,* hard and cruel and impossible, and he closed the distance between them as ruthlessly as he did anything else. Just as he'd done years ago on a dark street, in the deep shadows of a Spanish night. One hand slid over her hip to the small of her back, hauling her against the wall of his chest, even as his lips took control of hers, demanding she let him in, insisting she kiss him back.

And, God help her, she did.

She dropped her other shoe, she lost her mind, and she did.

It was so *hot. Finally,* a small voice whispered, insistent and jubilant. He tasted of lust and command and she was dizzy, so dizzy, she forgot herself.

She forgot everything but the heat of that mouth, the way he angled his head to kiss her more deeply, the way his palm on the small of her back pressed into her and in turn pressed her into the hard granite expanse of his lean chest. Her breasts felt too full and almost sore as they flattened against him, into him, and everywhere they touched felt like a fever, and she was kissing him back because he tasted like sorcery and for one brief, searing, shocking moment she wanted nothing more than to lose herself in an incantation she could hardly understand.

But she *wanted.* She *wanted* almost more than she

had ever wanted anything else, the inexorable pull of his mouth, his taste, *him,* roaring through her, altering her, changing everything—

He broke the kiss to mutter something harsh in Spanish, and reality slammed back into Dru. So hard she was distantly amazed her bones hadn't shattered from the impact.

She shoved against his chest blindly, and was entirely too aware not only that he chose to let her go, but that it was as if her very blood sang out to stay exactly where she was, plastered against him, just as she'd done once before and to her own detriment.

She staggered back a foot, then another. She was breathing too hard, teetering on the edge of a terrible panic, and she was afraid it would take no more than the faintest brush of wind to toss her right over into its grip. She could see nothing through the haze that seemed to cover her vision but that hooded, dangerous, dark amber gaze of his and that mouth—*that mouth*—

She should know better. She *did* know better. She could feel hysteria swell in her, indistinguishable from the lump in her throat and the clamoring of her pulse. Her stomach twisted and for a terrifying moment she didn't know if she was going to be sick or faint or some horrifying combination thereof.

But she sucked in another breath, and that particular crisis passed, somehow. He still only watched her. As if he knew exactly how hard her blood pumped through her body and where it seemed to pool. As if he knew exactly how much her breasts ached, and where they'd hardened. As if he knew how she burned for him, and always had.

Dru couldn't stand it. She couldn't stand *here.* So she turned on her bare heel, and bolted from the salon.

She picked up speed as she moved, aware as she began to run up the grand stairway toward the deck that she was breathing so heavily she might as well be sobbing. Maybe she was.

You little fool, some voice kept intoning in her head. *You're nothing but a latter-day Miss Havisham and twice as sad—*

She blinked in the bright slap of sunshine when she burst out onto the deck, momentarily blinded. She looked over her shoulder when she could see and he was right there, as she knew he would be, lean and dark and those hot, demanding eyes that looked almost gold in the Adriatic sunshine.

"Where are you going?" He was taunting her, those wicked brows of his raised. That mouth—*God, that mouth*— "I thought you didn't care about a little kiss?"

It's the devil or the deep blue sea, she thought, aware that she was almost certainly hysterical now. But her heart was already broken. She couldn't take anything more. She couldn't survive this again. She wasn't sure she'd survived it the first time, come to that.

Dru simply turned back around, took a running start toward the side of the yacht one story up from the sea, and jumped.

CHAPTER THREE

SHE had actually thrown herself off the side of the damned boat.

Cayo stood at the rail and scowled down at her as she surfaced in the water below and started swimming for the far-off shore, fighting to keep his temper under control. Fighting to shove all of that need and lust back where it belonged, shut down and locked away in the deepest recesses of his memory.

How had this happened? *Again?*

And yet he was all too aware there was no one to blame but himself. Which only made it worse.

"Is that *Dru?*" The voice that came from slightly behind him was shocked.

"'Dru?'" Cayo echoed icily.

He didn't want to know she had a casual nickname. He didn't want to think of her as a person. He didn't want this intoxicating taste of her in his mouth again, or this insane longing for her that stormed through him, making him so hard it bordered on the painful and, moreover, a stranger to himself. *He didn't want any of this.* But that dark drum that he told himself was only temper beat ever hotter inside of him, making him a liar yet again.

"I mean Miss Bennett, of course," the crew mem-

ber beside him, the head steward if Cayo was not mistaken, all but stammered. "Forgive me, sir, but has
she...fallen? Shouldn't we go and help her?"

"That is an excellent question," Cayo muttered.

He watched her for a long, tense moment, out there
in the blue sweep of water, her strokes long and sure.
He was very nearly forced to admire the willfulness
and sheer bloody-mindedness she'd displayed today.
Was still displaying, in fact. To say nothing of her
grace and skill in the water, even fully dressed. He
had to fight with himself to get his body under control, to force away the thick, near-liquid desire that
still pumped through him and *that thing* in him that
was far too alert now and would not have stopped at
that kiss. Oh, no. That had been the sort of kiss that
started scorching affairs, and had it not been Drusilla,
he would not even have thought twice—he would have
taken her there and then, on the floor of the salon if
necessary.

And up against the wall. And down among the soft
pillows in the seating area. And again and again, just
to test all that shocking chemistry that had blown up
around them—that he had told himself he'd forgotten
entirely until it was all he could think of all over again.
Just to see what they could make of it.

But it *was* Drusilla.

Cayo had always been a practical man. Deliberate
and focused in all he did. He had never varied from
the path he'd set himself; he'd never been tempted to
try. Except for one unfortunate slip in Cadiz that night,
and a repeat here on this yacht today.

That was two slips too many. And it was quite
enough. He had to get himself back under control and
stay there.

He watched as she flipped over to her back in the water, no doubt checking for any potential pursuit, and fought with that part of him that suggested he simply leave her there. She had already wasted too much of his time. His schedule had been packed full today, and he'd shoved it all aside so he could try to keep her from leaving. Why had he done any of this? And then kissed her?

It didn't matter, he told himself ruthlessly. She was too valuable to him as his assistant to risk her drowning, of course. Or to become his lover, as his body was still enthusiastically demanding. He'd decided the same thing three years ago when she'd applied for that promotion. He'd determined that she should stay exactly where she was and everything should remain exactly as it had been before they'd gone to Spain. He still didn't see why anything should change, when it had all been so perfect for so long, save two kisses that shouldn't have happened in the first place.

He didn't understand why she wanted to leave his employ so desperately, or why she was so furious with him all of a sudden. But he felt certain that if he threw enough money at the problem, whatever it was and especially if it was no more than her hurt feelings, she would find that it went away. His mouth twisted. People always did.

"Sir? Perhaps one of the motorboats? Only she's got a bit far out, now…?" the steward asked again, sounding simultaneously more subservient and more worried than he had before, a feat that might have amused Cayo had he not still been so at odds with his own temper.

He did not care for the feeling—uncertain and off-balance. He did not like the fact that Drusilla made him feel at all, much less like that. She was the perfect personal assistant, competent and reliable. And impersonal. It was when he saw her as a woman that he ran into trouble. He started to feel the way he imagined other, lesser men felt. Unsure. Even needy. Wholly unlike himself and all he stood for. It horrified him unto his very bones.

Never again, he'd vowed when he was still so young. *No more feelings.* He'd felt far too much in the first eighteen years of his life, and done nothing but suffer for it. He'd decided he was finished with it—that succumbing to such things was for the kind of man he had no intention of ever becoming. Weak. Malleable. Common. He refused to be any of those things, ever again.

And he'd let that drive him for nearly two decades. If something was out of his reach, he simply extended his reach and then took it anyway. If it was not for sale, he applied pressure until it turned out it was after all—and often at a lesser price thanks to his machinations. If a woman did not want him, he simply took pains to shower her with her heart's desire, whatever that might be, until she decided that perhaps she'd been too hasty in her initial rejection. If a bloody assistant wanted to leave his employ, he simply replaced her, and if he felt she should stay, he gave her whatever she wanted so that she did. He bought whatever he desired, because he could. Because he would never again be that little boy, marked with his mother's shame, expected to amount to little more than the sin that had made him. Because he did not, could not, and would not *care.*

Not that he did now, he assured himself. Not really. But whatever this was inside him—with its deep claws and driving lust, with its mad obsession over a woman who had tried to leave him twice today already—it was too close. Much closer than it should have been. It pumped in his blood. It made him hard. It made him *want*.

It was outrageous. He refused to allow it any more traction. *He refused.*

"Ready one of the motorboats," he said in a low voice, and heard a burst of action behind him, as if the yacht's entire staff had been poised on a knife's edge, waiting to hear the order. "I will fetch her myself."

He detected a note of surprise in the immediate affirmative answer he received, because, of course, he was Cayo Vila. Something he had clearly lost sight of today. He did not collect women or employees, they were delivered to him, like any other package. And yet here he was, chasing after this woman. Again. It was impossible, inconceivable—and even so, he was doing it.

So there was really only one question. Was he going out to drag her back onto the yacht and continue to tolerate this ridiculous little bit of theater until he got what he wanted? Or was he going out there to drown her with his bare hands, thereby solving the problem once and for all?

At the moment, he thought, his narrowed gaze on her determined figure as it made its stubborn way through the sea, away from him, he had no idea.

"Are you going to get in the boat? Or are you so enjoying your swim that you plan to make a night of it?" Cayo snapped from the comfortable bench seat in the chic little motorboat where he lounged, all dark and dangerous above her.

Dru ignored him. Or tried, anyway.

"It is further to the shore than it looks," he continued

in that same clipped tone. That mouth of his crooked in one corner, though there was nothing at all like a smile about it. "Not to mention the current. If you are not careful, you might very well find yourself swept all the way to Egypt."

Dru kept swimming, feeling entirely too close to grim. Or was that *defeated?* Had she truly kissed him like that? *Again?* Cadiz had been one thing. He had been so different that night, and it had seemed so organic, so excusable, given the circumstances. But there was no excuse for what had happened today. She knew how little he thought of her. *She knew.* And still, she'd kissed him *like that.* Wanton and wild. Aching and demanding and hot—

She would never forgive herself.

"Egypt would be far preferable to another moment spent in your company—" she threw at him, but he cut her off simply by clicking his fingers at the steward who operated the sleek little vessel for him. The engine roared to life, drowning out whatever she might have said next.

Dru stopped swimming then and trod water, watching in consternation and no little annoyance as the small craft looped around her, leaving her to bob helplessly in a converging circle of its wake. She got a slap of seawater in the face, and had to scrub at her eyes to clear them. When she opened them again, the engine had gone quiet once more and the boat was much too close. Again. Which in turn meant that *he* was much too close. How could she be in the middle of the sea and still feel so trapped? So hemmed in?

"You look like a raccoon," he said in his blunt, rude way. As if he was personally offended by it.

"Oh," she replied, her voice brittle. "Did you expect that I would maintain a perfectly made-up face while swimming for my life? Of course you did. I doubt you even know what mascara *is*. That it requires application and does not, in fact, magically appear to adorn the eyelashes of whatever woman happens to gaze upon you."

It took far more strength than it should have to keep from rubbing at her eyes again, at the mascara that had no doubt slid off her own lashes to coat her cheeks. *It doesn't matter,* she snapped at herself, and found she was surprised and faintly appalled at the force of her own vanity.

"I don't want to think about your mascara or your made-up face," he replied in that deceptively smooth voice of his, the one that made her bones seem to go soft inside her skin. "I want to pretend this day never happened and that I never had to see beyond the perfectly serene mask you normally wear."

"Whilst I, Mr. Vila, could not possibly care less about what you want."

That amused him. She could see his version of laughter move across that fierce, fascinating face, a kind of light over darkness. She had to swallow against her own reaction, and told herself it was the sea. The salt. The exertion. Not him. Not the aftereffects of a kiss that the water should have long since washed away.

God, she was such a terrible liar.

"What you do and do not care about," he replied in a voice gone smooth and sharp, like finely honed steel, "are among the great many things I do not want to know about you." His hard mouth crooked into a cold, predatory version of a smile. Dru would have preferred to come face-to-face with a shark, frankly. She reckoned she would have had far more of a chance.

"I know you are perfectly capable of discerning my meaning, Miss Bennett. I'll wait."

Dru was treading water again, and while the words she wanted to hurl at him crowded on her tongue, she gulped them back down, a bit painfully, and reviewed her situation. The truth was, she was tired. Exhausted. She had used up all her energy surviving these last years; she had precious little of it left, and what she did have she'd wasted on this contest of wills with Cayo today.

As if to underscore that thought, another wave crashed into her face, making her choke slightly and then duck down beneath the water. Where, for just a second, she could float beneath the surface and let herself feel how broken she was. How battered. Torn apart by this confusing day. By the long years that had preceded it. By kisses that never should have happened and the brother who never should have left her like this. She felt her body convulse as if she was sobbing there, underwater. As if she was finally giving in to it all.

It had been too much. Five long years of worrying and working and imagining bright futures that she'd never quite believed in. Not fully. But she'd tried. When Dominic was free of his addictions, she'd told herself. When she worked so hard because she wanted to, not because she had to. She'd dreamed hard, and convinced herself it could happen if she only worked hard enough. She'd dreamed her way out of her rotten childhood into something brighter, hadn't she? Why not this, too?

And then had come that terrible day when she'd received the news that Dominic was dead. She'd had to trail Cayo through a manufacturing plant in Belgium, acting as if her heart hadn't been ripped from her body and stamped into oblivion half the world away, not that

Cayo had noticed any difference. Not that she'd let him see it. She'd made certain that all of Dominic's bills and debts were paid, while a squat and encompassing grief hunkered down on her, waiting. Just waiting. She'd ignored that, too. She'd reasoned it was her *job* to ignore it, to pretend she was perfectly fine. She'd taken pride in her ability to be perfect for Cayo. To fulfill his needs no matter what was happening to her.

Reading that email early this morning in London and seeing her years with Cayo for the sham they really were had landed the killing blow. It was the final straw. And part of her wanted simply to sink like a stone now, deep into the embrace of the Adriatic, and be done with all of this. Just let it all go. Hadn't Dominic done the same, at the end of the day? Why shouldn't she? What was she holding on to, anyway?

But Cayo would think it was all about him, wouldn't he? She knew he would. And she couldn't allow that. She simply couldn't.

She kicked, hard, and shot back up to the surface and the sun, pulling in a ragged breath as her gaze focused on Cayo. He still sat there, noticeably irritated, as if it was no matter to him whether she sank or swam, only that she was disrupting his afternoon.

Somehow, that was galvanizing.

She would not go under again, she understood then, as she stared up at him, at this man to whom she'd sacrificed herself, day in and day out, thanks to her own rich fantasy life. She would not break, not for Cayo, not for anything.

How could she? She was already broken.

And there was a strength in that, she thought, wiping the water from her face and pretending she didn't feel a heat beneath her eyes that indicated it was not entirely the sea she was scrubbing away.

I promise you, Dominic, she thought fiercely, her own little prayer, *I will walk away from this man at long last and I will take you to Bora Bora the way you always wanted. I'll give you to the wind and the water the way I swore I would. And then we'll both be free.*

So she swallowed back the bitter words she would have liked to throw out to make herself feel better about just how much of a fool she'd been and swam over to the side of the boat. She reached up to grip the edge of it. Cayo shifted, moving that taut, tense body of his even closer. He was more furious than she'd ever seen him. She could feel it as easily as she felt the sun far above, the sea all around.

"Fine," she said, tilting her head to look up at him as if none of that bothered her in the least. "I'll get in the boat."

"I know you will," he agreed silkily. *Furiously,* she thought. "But while I have you here, Miss Bennett, let's talk terms, shall we?"

Dru let go of the gunwale with one hand and used it to slick her hair back from her face. The twist she'd carefully created this morning in London was long gone now, and she imagined that the dark mass of her hair hung about her like seaweed. Happily, she was certain that Cayo would deeply disapprove of it. That little kick of pleasure allowed her to simply raise her brows at him and wait. As if none of this hurt her. As if *he* didn't hurt her at all.

"I imagine that this entire display was a calculated effort to get me to recognize that you are, in fact, a person," he said in that insufferable way of his, so very patronizing, that Dru would not have been at all surprised if it had left marks.

"How good of you to ignore almost everything I actually said," she murmured in a similar tone, even as she eyed him warily.

"I will double your salary," he told her as if he hadn't heard her.

Dru was forced to calculate how very much money it was that he was offering her, and wonder, for the briefest treacherous second, if it was truly necessary to escape him… But of course it was. She could stay with him, or she could have her self-respect, whatever was left of it. She couldn't have both. Today had certainly proved that.

There were so many things she wanted to say, but the way he looked at her made Dru suspect that if she said any of them, he would leave her in the water. She knew exactly how ruthless he could be. So she only held on to the side of the small motorboat, bobbing gently along with it in the rise and fall of the waves, and watched him.

"I'm cold," she said crisply, because there were minefields in every other thing she might have thought to say. "Are you going to help me into the boat?"

There was a brief, intense sort of moment, and then he leaned over, slid his hands beneath her arms, and hoisted her up and out of the water as if she weighed no more than a child. Water sluiced from her wet clothes as her feet came down against the slippery bottom of the small boat, and she was suddenly aware of too many things. The sodden fabric of her skirt, ten times heavier than it should have been, wrapped much too tightly around her hips and thighs. The slick wetness of her blouse as it flattened against her skin in the sea breeze. The heavy tangle of her wet hair, tumbling this way and that in a disastrous mess. All of which made her feel much too cold, and, oddly, something very much like vulnerable.

But then she looked up, and the air seemed to empty out of her lungs. And she did not have to see his eyes to know that he was staring at the way her soaking-wet clothes molded to her curves, and, a quick glance down confirmed, left nothing at all to the imagination. Her blouse had been a soft gray when dry, but wet it was nearly translucent, and showed off the bright magenta bra she'd worn beneath.

Dru couldn't process the kaleidoscope of emotion that shifted through her then: chagrin, embarrassment, that horrible vulnerability, those underwater sobs threatening to spill out once again. She looked longingly at the sea once more, and if she hadn't been so cold she might well have tossed herself right back into it.

"Don't even think about it," he gritted out, and then several things happened simultaneously.

The boat lurched forward, no doubt in response to some signal of Cayo's, and Dru would have toppled against him had he not grabbed her around the waist and deposited her on the pristine white cushions next to him. She had the impression of his strength and heat, and there was that wild, desperate surge of desire inside of her that made her hate herself anew, and then she was sitting beside him as the boat headed toward the boarding deck of the great yacht, wet skirt itchy and awful against her and her hair flying madly in the wind.

Cayo did not speak again until they were safely back on board, and one of his silent and expressionless crew members had draped a very warm, very large towel over her shoulders. She aimed a grateful smile at the head steward as she wrapped the soft towel tight around her, and then felt very much like the poster child for *Les Misérables* when she directed her attention back toward her former employer. Pathetic and bedraggled whilst Cayo, naturally, gazed down at her like some kind of untouchable Spanish god, all of his dangerous beauty gleaming in the last of the day's sun.

The crew members disappeared as if they could see the coming storm closing in on them. If she had had any sense at all, she would have done the same. Instead she stood there and waited, her back straight as a ruler and her expression, she hoped, as serene as possible when she was still so wet and wrecked. Cayo slid his sunglasses down his haughty blade of a nose and regarded her with a glint in those dark gold eyes that should have cowed her at fifty paces—and he was much closer than that.

"I'm sure you know precisely where there are extra clothes on this yacht," he said quietly. She didn't trust that tone. It suggested great horrors lurking beneath it. "I suggest you avail yourself of them. Then come find me. We will behave like civilized, professional people. We will discuss the terms of your continued employment in more detail. And we will pretend that the rest of this day never happened."

Dru forced a smile. She told herself she was entirely uncowed.

"I was cold and wanted to get out of the water," she said. "I'm still quitting." She shrugged at his incredulous expression. "I can either tell you what you want to hear and then disappear at the first available opportunity, or I can be honest about it and hope you'll let me leave with some dignity. Your choice."

He was looking at her as if he had long since destroyed her with the force of that incinerating gaze alone, and was looking at some ash remnant where she'd once stood. She gazed back at him, and told herself the goose bumps were only from the cold.

"Surely we left dignity far behind today, you and I," he said in a very low voice that seemed to shiver through her, or maybe she simply shivered in response, she couldn't tell.

"Your choice remains the same," she managed to say as if she hadn't noticed. As if it didn't matter. As if this was easy for her and she didn't feel something far too much like a sob, like despair, clogging the back of her throat. "Dignity or no."

For a moment, there was no sound but the ocean breeze, and the waves against the hull of the yacht.

"Go clean yourself up, Miss Bennett," Cayo said then, so softly, dark and menacing and his accent too intense to be anything but furious, and it all should have scared her. It really should have, had there been any part of her left unbattered. Unbroken. "And we'll talk."

But when Dru walked into the luxurious, dark-wood-paneled and chandeliered study that was part of his expansive master suite some time later, she was not, she knew very well, "cleaned up" in the way that he'd expected. He was standing at his desk with his mobile phone clamped to his ear, talking in the brusque tone that indicated he was tending to some or other facet of his business. She could probably have figured out which facet, had she wanted to, had she listened attentively as she would have done automatically before—but she didn't want to do any of the things she'd done before, did she? They'd all led her here. So instead, she simply waited.

And she wasn't surprised when he turned to look at her and paused. Then scowled.

"I must go," he said into the phone and ended the call with a jerk of his hand, all without taking his eyes from her.

A stark, strained moment passed, then another.

"What the hell are you wearing?" he asked.

"I was unaware there was a dress code I was expected to follow," she replied as if she didn't understand him. "The last woman I saw on this boat, only an hour or so ago, appeared to be wearing dental floss as a fashion statement."

"She is no longer with us," he said, his eyes narrow and hostile, "but that does not explain why you are dressed as if you are..." His voice actually trailed away.

"A normal person?" she asked. She'd known he would not like what she wore, hadn't she? She'd chosen these clothes deliberately. She could admit that much. "Come now, Mr. Vila. This is the twenty-first century. This can't be the first time you've seen a woman in jeans."

"It is the first time I have seen *you* in jeans." His voice was hard then, as hard as the way he was looking at her. As hard as the way her pulse seemed to jump beneath her skin. It made goose bumps rise on her arms. "But I had no idea your hair was so..." Whatever flared in his gaze then made Dru's skin seem to stretch tight and then shrink into her. "Long."

Dru shrugged as if she was completely unfazed by him and moved farther into the room, settling herself on one of the plush armchairs that was angled for the best sea view through the broad windows. He had been right—she knew where all the extra clothes were stored. All the items that Cayo kept stocked for any unexpected female guests as well as the skeleton wardrobe he kept for both her and him should his business bring them here by surprise.

And by "Cayo kept stocked" she meant, of course, that she did.

After she'd washed away the sea and her own self-destructive reaction to him throughout this long day, particularly that mind-numbing kiss, she had toweled off and then opened up the little emergency suitcase that she'd had installed in the offices and residences he visited most often, scattered here and there across the globe.

Inside the case, a conservative gray suit was pressed in plastic, with two blouses to choose from, one in a pale pink and one in an understated taupe, and a change of underthings in non-racy, uninteresting beige. She'd packed pins for her hair and the proper tools to tame the wavy mess of it into professional sleekness. There was a small bag of her preferred toiletries and another of her basic cosmetics. There were sensible shoes that would go with anything and a black cashmere cardigan in case she'd felt called to appear "casual." She'd even packed away an assortment of accessories, all conservatively stylish, so she could look as pulled together as she always did even if she'd found herself on board thanks to one of Cayo's last-minute whims. She'd packed everything, in other words, that she could possibly need to climb right back into her role as his handy robot without so much as an unsightly wrinkle.

And she hadn't been able to bring herself to do it.

Instead, she'd let her hair dry naturally as she'd taken her time dressing, and now it hung in dark waves down her back. She'd found a pair of white denim jeans in one closet, much more snug than she liked, which was only to be expected given the gazelle-like proportions of most of his usual female guests, and a lovely palazzo top in a vibrant blue-and-white pattern in another, which was loose and flowy and balanced out the jeans. She'd tossed on a slate-gray wrap to guard against the sea air now that evening was upon them and the temperature had dropped, and had left her feet and her face entirely bare.

She looked like…herself. At last. Yet Cayo stared at her as if she were a ghost.

"Is this another version of throwing yourself overboard, Miss Bennett?" he asked, his voice a lash across the quiet room. It made her heart leap into a wild gallop in her chest. "Another desperate bid for my attention?"

"You are the one who wanted to talk, not me," she replied, summoning a cold smile from somewhere though she didn't feel cold at all. Not when she was near him. No matter what he did. "I would have been perfectly happy to remove myself from the glare of your attention. For good."

That muscle in his lean jaw moved, but nothing else did. He was like a stone carving of simmering rage.

"What if I triple your salary?" His voice was cold and yet grim, his dark eyes flat and considering. "Did you say you lived in a leased bedsit? I'll buy you a flat. A penthouse, if you like. Pick the London neighborhood you prefer."

So much of her longed to do it. Who wouldn't? He was offering her an entirely different life. A very, very good life, at the price of a job she'd always liked well enough, until today.

But…then what? she asked herself. Wasn't what he suggested really no more than a sterile form of prostitution, when all was said and done? Give herself over to him, and he would pay for it. And she would do it, she knew with a hollow, painful sort of certainty, not because it made financial sense, not because she stood to gain so much—but because she longed for him. Because he would be using her skills and she would be dreaming about *one more night* like the one in Cadiz. *One more kiss* like the one today. What would become of her after five more years of this? Ten? She'd put Miss Havisham to shame in her bought-and-paid-for London flat, tarting herself up every day in her corporate costume to better please him, his favorite little automaton….

She could see it all too clearly and it made her feel sick. It would be easier if she could simply do it for the money, the way she had when this had started. But she was too far gone. At least, she thought now, she knew it. Surely that was something. A first step.

"I don't want to live in London," she told him. She lifted a shoulder and then dropped it. She ignored the way her stomach twisted, and that howling, broken-hearted part of her that wanted him any way she could have him. Even now. Even like this. "I don't want a flat."

"Where, then?" He raised a brow. "Are you angling for a house? An estate? A private island? I think I have all of the above."

"Indeed you do," she replied. It was almost comforting to pull up all of that information she knew about him and his many and varied assets—until she remembered how deeply proud she'd always been that she so rarely had to consult the computer to access Cayo's details. It was yet more evidence of how deeply pathetic she was. "You have sixteen residential properties, some of which are also estates. You also own three private islands, as well as a modest collection of atolls. That's at last count. You do always seem to acquire more, don't you?"

Cayo leaned back against the wide desk that stretched across the center of the room as if it were a throne he expected to be worshipped upon and crossed his arms over his chest, and she couldn't deny the intensity of that midnight stare. She felt it like fire, down to the bare soles of her feet. Her toes curled slightly in response, and she flexed her feet to stop it. And still he merely watched her, that gaze of his dark and stirring, and she had no idea what he saw.

"Pick one." It was a command.

"You can't buy me back," she said, her own voice just as quiet as his. Just as deliberate. "I don't want your money."

"Everyone has a price, Miss Bennett." He rubbed at his jaw with one hand, a considering light in his unnerving eyes. "Especially those who claim they do not, I usually find."

"Yes," she said, shifting in her chair as a kind of restlessness swirled through her. She wanted to fast forward through this, desperately. She wanted to be on the other side of it, when she'd already found the strength to defy him, had walked away and was living without him. She wanted this done already; she didn't want to *do* it. "I know how you operate. But I have no family left to threaten or save. No outstanding debts you can leverage to your advantage. No deep, dark secrets you can threaten to expose or offer to hide more deeply. Nothing at all that can force me to take a job I don't want, I'm afraid."

He only watched her in that way of his, as if it made no difference what she said to him. Because, she realized, it didn't. Not to him. He was immoveable. A wall. And maybe he even enjoyed watching her batter herself against the sheer iron of his will. She wouldn't put anything past him. Desperation coursed through her then, a hectic surge of electricity, and Dru couldn't sit still any longer. She got to her feet and then eased away from him, as if by standing she'd ceded ground to him.

"Miss Bennett," he began in a voice she recognized. It was the voice he used to mollify his victims before he felled them with a killing blow. She knew it all too well. She'd heard it in a hundred board rooms. In a thousand conference calls.

She couldn't take it here, now. Aimed directly at her.

"Just stop!" she heard herself cry out. There was an inexorable force moving through her, despair and desperation swelling large, and she couldn't seem to do anything but obey it. She faced him again, her hands balling into fists while a scalding heat threatened the back of her eyes. "Why are you doing this?"

"I told you," he said impatiently, so cold and forbidding and *annoyed* while she fell into so many pieces before him. "You are the best personal assistant I've ever had. That is not a compliment. It is a statement of fact."

"That might be true," she managed to say, fighting to keep the swirl of emotion inside her to herself. "But it doesn't explain this." When he shifted his weight as if he meant to argue, because of course he did, he always did, she threw up her hands as if she could hold him off. "You could replace me with fifteen perfect assistants, a fleet of them trained and ready to serve you within the hour. You could replace me with anyone in the entire world if you chose. There is absolutely no reason for any of this—not three years ago and not now!"

"Apparently," he said coldly, "your price is higher than most."

"It's insane." She shook her hair back from her face, ordered herself not to burst into tears. "You don't need me."

"But I want you." Harsh. Uncompromising.

And not at all in the way she wanted him. That was perfectly plain.

It was as if something burst inside of her.

"You will never understand!" She stopped trying to hold herself back, to keep herself in check. What was the point? "There was someone I *loved*. Someone I lost. Years I can never get back." She didn't care that her voice was as shaky as it was loud, that her eyes were wet. She didn't care what he might see when he looked at her, or worry that he might suspect she was talking about more than her brother. She had given herself permission to do this, hadn't she? This was what *flappable* looked like. "There is no amount of money you can offer me that can fix the things that are broken. Nothing that can give me back what I lost—what was taken from me. *Nothing*." Nor, worse, what she'd given him, fool that she was. She heaved a ragged breath and kept on. "I want to disappear into a world where Cayo Vila doesn't matter, to me or anyone else."

She wanted that last bit most of all.

And in a cutting bit of unwelcome self-awareness, she accepted the sad truth of things. He didn't have to offer her flats or estates or islands. He didn't have to throw his money at her.

If he'd said he wanted her and meant, for once, that he wanted *her*...

If, even now, he'd pulled her close and told her that he simply couldn't imagine his life without her...

There was that little masochist within, Dru knew all too well, who would work for him for free, if only he wanted her like that.

But Cayo didn't want anyone like that. Especially not her. She could tell herself he was incapable of it, that he'd never known love and never would—but that was no more than a pretty gloss on the same ugly truth. She understood all of that.

And still, she yearned for him.

"You have made your point," he said, after a strained moment.

"Then, please. Let me go." It was harder to choke out than it should have been. She hated herself for that, too.

For a moment she thought he might, and her stomach dropped. *Disbelief,* she lied to herself.

There was that odd light in his fascinating eyes—but then his face seemed to shutter itself and darken, and he straightened to his full height, the better to look down at her. And she reminded herself that this was Cayo Vila, and he let nothing go. He never bent. He never compromised. He simply kept on going until he won.

She couldn't understand why she couldn't seem to breathe.

"You owe me two weeks," he said, as if he were rendering a prison sentence. "I intend to have them. You can do your job for those two weeks and fulfill your contractual obligations to me, or I'll simply keep you with me like a dog on a leash, purely out of spite."

But he didn't look spiteful. He looked something far closer to sad, and it made her stomach twist. Again.

And that terrible longing swelled again inside her, making her ache. Making her wish—but her wishes were dangerous, and they tore her into tatters every time. She shoved them aside.

Cayo smiled, as if from far away, hard and wintry. "Your choice, Miss Bennett."

CHAPTER FOUR

HE should have been happy—or at the very least, satisfied.

Cayo lounged back against his chair and gazed around the white-linen-draped table that stretched the length of the formal dining room in the Presidential Suite of the Hotel Principe di Savoia in Milan, surveying the small dinner he'd had Drusilla throw here in one of Europe's most prestigious spaces. The rooms of the vast suite gave the impression of belonging to royalty perhaps, so stunning were they, all high ceilings, carefully selected antiques and the finest Italian craftsmanship on display at every turn. Wealth and elegance seemed to shimmer up from the very floors to dance in the air around them.

The investors were duly impressed, as expected. They smoked cigars and let out loud belly laughs over the remains of the last of the seven courses they'd enjoyed. Their pleasure seemed to ricochet off the paneled mahogany walls and gleam forth from the impressive Murano glass chandeliers that hung above them, in resplendent reds and blues, and would no doubt be reflected in the size of their investments, as planned. This would be another success, Cayo knew without the smallest doubt. More money, more power for the Vila Group.

And yet all he could seem to concentrate on tonight was Drusilla.

"Fine," she had thrown at him on the yacht, those gray eyes of hers both furious and something far darker, her mouth very nearly trembling in a way that had made him feel restless. Unsettled. "I'm not going to play this game with you any longer. If you want your two weeks, you'll have them—but that's the end of it."

"Two weeks as my assistant or my pet," he'd reiterated. "I don't care which."

She'd laughed, and it was a hollow sound. "I hate you."

"That bores me," he'd replied, his gaze hard on hers. "And furthermore, makes you but one among a great many."

"By that you mean, I imagine, the entire world?" she'd sniped at him. Her tone, the way she was standing there with her hands in fists—it had made him suspicious.

"I'd suggest you think twice before you attempt to sabotage me in some passive-aggressive display in your last days with me, Miss Bennett," he'd cautioned her, and the look she'd turned on him then should have flayed him alive. Perhaps it had. "You won't like the result."

"Don't worry, *Mr. Vila*," she'd said, his name a low, dark curse, hitting him in ways he didn't fully understand. "When I decide to sabotage you, there will be nothing in the least bit passive about it."

She'd stalked away from him that afternoon, and he hadn't seen her again until the following morning, when she'd presented herself in his suite at breakfast, dressed in the perfectly unremarkable sort of professional clothes she usually wore. No skintight white jeans licking over her long legs to taunt him and remind him how they'd once clenched over his hips. No wild gypsy hair to shatter his concentration and invade his dreams. She'd sat herself in a chair with her tablet on her lap, and had asked him, as she'd done a thousand times before, with no particular inflection or agenda, if his plans for the day deviated from his written schedule.

As if the previous day had never happened.

If he didn't know better, he thought now, watching her through narrowed eyes, he could almost imagine that nothing had changed between them at all. That she had never quit, that he had never forced her into giving him her contracted two weeks.

That they had never kissed like that, nor let their tempers flare, revealing too many things he found he did not wish to think about, and too much heat besides.

Almost.

Tonight she looked as professional and cool as ever, with the prettiness he could no longer seem to ignore an enviable accent to her quiet competence. She wore a simple blue sheath dress with a tailored jacket that trumpeted her restrained and capable form of elegance, her trademark. She operated as his right hand in situations like this, his secret weapon, making it seem as if he was not giving a presentation designed to result in lavish investments so much as sharing a fascinating opportunity with would-be friends.

She made him seem far more engaging and charming than he was, he'd concluded over the course of the long evening, and wondered how he'd never seen that quite so clearly before. She gave him that human touch that so many furious and defeated rivals claimed he lacked.

He'd watched her do it tonight—lighting up the carefully selected group of ten investors with her attention, making them talk about themselves, letting them each feel interesting and important. *Valued.* She hung on their words, anticipated their questions, soothed them and laughed with them in turn, all of it in that cool, intelligent way of hers that seemed wholly authentic instead of cloying. They ate her up.

And because of her, Cayo could simply be his ruthless, focused self, and no one felt overly intimidated or defensive.

She sat at the far end of the lavishly appointed table now, her tablet in her hand as always, periodically tapping into it as she fielded questions and tended to the various needs of everyone around her. She made it look so easy. She was smooth and matter-of-fact, as if it was only natural that the French businessman should demand a Reiki massage at two in the morning and it *delighted* her to be able to contact the concierge on his behalf. She was his walking computer, his butler, and, if Cayo was honest, his true second-in-command. Smart, dependable, even trustworthy. He should have encouraged her to leave him three years ago when she'd wanted that promotion. She could have been running companies for him by now. She was that good.

Which was, of course, why he'd been so loath to let her do it.

Or one reason, anyway, he thought now, darkly impatient with himself. He idly fingered his wineglass as he half pretended to pay attention to the conversation that swelled around him. Not that anyone expected him

to charm them, of course. Or even be particularly polite, for that matter. That was Drusilla's job.

She is magnificent, he thought, and ignored the sudden pang that followed as he considered how soon she
would be gone. How soon he would have to think up a
new approach, a new game to get what he wanted from
investors like this without her deft touch, her quiet, almost invisible support.

And how soon he would have to face this stubborn
thing in him he didn't want to acknowledge: how little
he wanted her to leave, and his growing suspicion that
it was far less about business than he was comfortable
admitting. Even to himself.

"Trust me, Mr. Peck," he heard her say to the self-
satisfied gentleman on her left, heir to what remained
of a steel fortune in one of those smaller, ugly-named
American cities, making the man puff up as if she was
sharing a great confidence, "this is the sort of meal that
will change your life. Three Michelin stars, naturally.
I've made you a reservation for tomorrow at nine."

She straightened then, and her gaze met his down
the length of the table, with all of the investors and
cigar smoke and concentrated wealth in between them.
It was as if the rest of the room was plunged into darkness, as if it ceased to exist entirely, and there was
nothing but Drusilla. Nothing but the searing impact
of their connection. And he saw the truth on that pretty
face of hers he could now read far too well. He felt
it kick in him, as if she'd reached across the table,
over the remnants of the feast they'd all shared and
the money they'd won, and landed a vicious blow with
the nearest blunt object. A hard one, directly into his
solar plexus.

She hated him. He hadn't thought much of it when

she'd said it, as so many people had said the same over the years that it was like so much white noise. But he was beginning to believe she actually meant it. And more, that she thought he was a monster.

None of that was new. None of it was surprising. But this was: he knew full well he'd acted like one.

He'd do well to remember that.

Much later that night, the investors were finally gone, off to their own debaucheries or beds or both, and Cayo found he couldn't sleep.

He prowled through the suite's great room, hardly noticing the opulence surrounding him, from the paintings that graced the walls of the vast, airy space to the hand-blown light fixtures at every turn and breathtaking antiques littered about. He pushed his way out onto the terrace that wrapped around the suite, offering commanding views across Milan. The spires of the famous Duomo in the city center pierced the night, lit up against the wet, faintly chilly dark. On a clear day the Alps would be there in the distance, snowcapped and beautiful, and he had the fanciful notion he could sense them out there, looming and watchful. But he could see nothing at all but Drusilla. As if she haunted him, and she hadn't even left him yet.

Monster, he thought again, the word on a bitter loop in his head. *She thinks you are a monster.*

He didn't know why it mattered to him. Why it interfered with his rest. But here he was, scowling out at a sleeping city in the dead of night.

He couldn't stop running through the events of the past days in his head, and he hardly recognized himself in his own recollections. Where was his famous control, which made titans of industry cower before him? Where was the cool head that had always guided him so unerringly and that had caused more than one competitor to accuse him of being more machine than man? Why did he care so much about one assistant's resignation that he'd turned into...this creature who roared and threatened, and abducted her across the whole of Europe?

It was just as his grandfather had predicted so long ago, he thought, the long-forgotten memory surfacing against his will, still filled with all of the misery and pain of his youth. He moved to the edge of the terrace and stood there, unmindful of the wet air, the cold, the city spread out before him. And then he found himself thrust back in time and into the place in the world he liked the very least: his home. Or more precisely, the place he'd been born, and had left eighteen years later. For good.

The entire village had predicted he would come to nothing. He was born of sin and made of shame, they'd sneered, as often to his face as behind his back. Look at his mother! Look how she'd turned out! A whore abandoned and forced to spend the rest of her days locked away in a convent as penance. No one would have been at all surprised if his own life had followed the same path. No one would have thought twice if he'd ended up as disgraced and shunned as she had been before she'd disappeared behind the convent walls.

No one had expected Cayo Vila to be anything more than the stain he already was on his family's name.

In fact, that was all they expected of him. That was, the whole of the small village and his grandfather agreed, his destiny. His fate. That was what became of children like him, made in disgrace and summarily discarded by both his parents.

And yet, despite this, he had tried so hard. His lips curled now, remembering those empty, fruitless years. He'd wanted so badly to *belong,* since he'd first understood, as a small boy, that he did not. He'd obeyed his grandfather in all things. He'd excelled at school. He'd worked tirelessly in the family's small cobbler's shop, and he'd never complained, while other boys his age played *futbol* and roamed about, carefree. He'd never fought with those who threw slurs and insults his way—at least, he'd never been caught. He'd tried his best to prove with his every breath and word and deed that he was not deserving of the scorn and contempt that had been his birthright. He'd tried to show that he was blameless. That he belonged to the village, to his family, despite how he'd come to be there.

He'd really believed he could sway them. That old current of frustration moved through him then, as if it still had the power to hurt him. It didn't, he told himself. Of course it didn't. That would require a heart, for one thing, and he had done without his for more than twenty years. Deliberately.

"I have done my duty," his grandfather had said to him on the morning of his eighteenth birthday, almost before Cayo had been fully awake. As if he'd been unable to wait any longer, so great was the burden he'd carried all these years. "But you are now a man, and you must bear the weight of your mother's shame on your own."

Cayo remembered the look on his grandfather's stern face, so much like his own, the light in the dark eyes as they met his. It had been the first time in his life he'd ever seen the old man look anything close to happy.

"But, *abuelo*—" he had begun, thinking he could argue his case.

"You are not my grandson," the old man had said, that terrible note of finality in his voice. His grizzled old chin had risen with some kind of awful pride. "I have done what I must for you, and now I wash my hands of it. Never call me *abuelo* again."

And Cayo never had. Not when he'd made his first million. Not when he'd bought every piece of property in that godforsaken village, every house and every field, every shop and every building, by the time he was twenty-seven. Not even when he'd stood over the old man's bed in the hospital, and watched impassively as the man who had raised him—if that was what it could be called—breathed his last.

There had been no reconciliation. There had been no hint of regret, no last-moment reversals before death had come to claim the old man three years ago. Cayo had been thirty-three then, and a millionaire several times over. He had owned more things than he could count. A small Spanish village tucked away in the hills of Andalusia hardly registered.

He had not seen himself as any kind of stain on the village's heralded white walls as he'd been driven through the streets in the back of a Lexus, and he very much doubted that any of the villagers mistook him for one. They'd hardly dare, would they, given that he'd held their lives and livelihoods in his hand. He had not seen himself as having anything to do with the place, with the Cadiz province, Andalusia, or even Spain itself, for that matter. He had hardly been able to recall that he had ever lived there, much less felt anything at all for the small-minded people who had so disdained him—and were now compelled to call him landlord.

"Not you!" his grandfather had wheezed, surfacing from his final illness only briefly, only once, to stare at Cayo in horror. It had been some fifteen years. *"Ay dios mio!"*

"Me," Cayo had confirmed coldly, standing at the foot of the hospital bed.

The old man had crossed himself, his hands knotted with arthritis, frail and shaking. Cayo had been unmoved.

"The devil is in you," this man who shared his blood had croaked out, his voice a faint thread of sound in the quiet room. "It has always been in you."

"My apologies," Cayo had said. His voice had been dry. Almost careless. What could such a small, shriveled husk of a man do to him now? It had seemed almost like a dream that he had ever had the power to hurt Cayo. Much less that he had succeeded. "I was your duty then, and it seems I am now your curse."

As if he'd agreed entirely, the old man had not spoken another word. He'd only crossed himself again, and had soon thereafter slipped away.

And Cayo had felt absolutely nothing.

He hadn't let himself feel much of anything since he'd walked out of that village on his eighteenth birthday. On that day, he'd looked back. He'd mourned what he'd believed he'd lost. He'd *felt*. Betrayed. Discarded. All the many things a weak man—a boy—felt. And when he'd finally pulled himself together and accepted the fact that he was alone, that he'd never been anything but alone and never would be again, he'd brushed himself off and shut down the pathetic part of him that still clung to all those counterproductive *feelings*. He'd left his heart in the hill town of his youth, and he'd never had cause to regret that. Or, for that matter, notice its lack.

So he had felt nothing when he'd walked into the hall where Drusilla had waited, her expression carefully neutral as befitted a personal assistant well paid to have no reaction at all to anything in her boss's life. He'd felt nothing on the long drive back to his hotel in Cadiz City, down from the mountains with their Moorish villages and out toward the Costa de la Luz, like a trip through his own memories. He'd felt nothing throughout the rest of that long night, though the *manzanilla* had first loosened his tongue and then, later, had him kissing Drusilla against a wall in a narrow walkway in the old city, lifting her high against him so her legs wrapped around his hips, drowning himself in the honeyed heat of her mouth, her kiss.

Nothing at all.

Her lips had enchanted him, full and slick against his. And that lithe body, those sensual curves, the spellbinding slide of her against him. He was hard again, remembering it, as if he was still on that dark city street three years ago instead of in a chilly Milan night, here, now. And that treacherous heart he'd thought he'd trained to know better beat out a rhythm that made him question things he shouldn't. Made him *want* so hard, so deep, it began to feel more like *need*. He bit out a blistering Spanish curse that had no discernible effect at all, and rubbed his hands over his face.

Whatever this was, whatever terrible madness that was taking him over against his will and beyond his control, it had to stop.

Madre de Dios, but it had to.

* * *

Dru shivered as the cold air hit her, pulling her wrap tighter around her and wishing she'd dressed for bed in something more substantial than the champagne-colored silk pajamas the presidential suite's dedicated butler had produced along with the outfit she'd worn at the dinner. She'd been trying to sleep for hours. She'd been lying in her bedroom, glowering at all its opulence as if the gold-and-cream Empire-style chairs or gilt-edged scarlet chaise were to blame for her predicament.

Why had she given in to him? Why had she agreed to work through the two weeks he'd demanded? It had been two days since she'd backed down and she still couldn't answer herself. Not satisfactorily. Not in any way that didn't make her hate herself more. Finally, she'd given up, and decided to take in some fresh air.

Outside, the night was damp. The overcast sky made the darkness feel fuller, somehow, while the city lights twinkled softly all around. It was beautiful. Like everything Cayo touched, everything he did. Like Cayo himself. And as cold.

She'd stayed because it was the quickest, easiest solution, or so she'd spent the past two days telling herself. Escape from Cayo meant subjecting herself to this and really, what was two more weeks? It had been five years. Two weeks would fly by, and that would be the end of it. Done and dusted.

The problem was, she knew better. On some level, she was relieved. As if this was a reprieve. As if Cayo might come to his senses and redeem himself—

She despaired of herself and this faith she had in him, so desperately misplaced. She truly did. How could she trust herself to be strong enough to walk away from him again when it had been so hard the first time? What made her think she could really do it in two weeks' time when she'd failed so spectacularly now?

"If you throw yourself from a height like this, I think you'll find the Piazza della Repubblica will provide somewhat less of a cushion than the Adriatic," he said from the shadows, making Dru jump. She clapped her hands to her chest as if she could force her heart to stop its panicked clamoring, whirling around to gape at him as he bore down upon her. "All the king's horses and all the king's men, and so on."

He looked dark and brooding, and, as if to taunt her, distractingly, impossibly sexy. He wore a luxurious-looking navy silk robe he hadn't bothered to pull closed over the sort of male underclothes that clung black and tight to acres of his taut thighs, making him look like a heart-stopping combination of an underwear model and a king. Dru's mouth went dry. It was one thing when he swanned about in his five-thousand-pound suits. It was another when he wore what passed for casual attire, all of which seemed to emphasize his athleticism, his masculine grace. But this... This was something else.

This was a fantasy come to life. *Her* fantasy, in fact. Suddenly, she was acutely aware that she was hardly dressed, that the silk pajamas caressed her skin with every breath, that she felt more naked than if she'd actually been unclothed, somehow. She felt heat wash over her, then spread, the flush of it rolling all through her body, like his touch.

And it didn't matter how angry she was at him, how foolish she felt or how betrayed. In the middle of the night, on a terrace in Italy, Dru was forced to admit the fact that she had never truly got a handle on just how devastatingly attractive Cayo was, or how much it had always affected her. Even before that night in Cadiz City.

"I didn't know you were out here," she said, and she could hear it in her voice, that slight quaver that gave her away. That all but shouted the things she didn't want to admit to herself and certainly didn't want him to know. How she melted for him, even now. How she ached in all the places she wished he would touch her with those capable hands, that difficult, addicting mouth. Her lips, her breasts. And that hunger between her thighs.

It was as if the dark, or the late hour, made it impossible to lie to herself any longer.

He tilted his head very slightly to the side as he drew close, studying her face. He'd been even colder and more distant than usual at dinner, prompting Dru to truly question her sanity and self-respect when she'd found herself *worrying* about him. What did that say about her, that even now, abducted and threatened and coerced, she took time out from her righteous indignation to worry about the man who'd done all of those things? *To her?*

Nothing good, she knew. Nothing healthy. No wonder she couldn't sleep.

"Here we are again in the dark," he said, a curious note in that deep voice of his. His face was even fiercer in the shadows, hardly lit up at all by the light spilling out from within, but still the dark amber of his eyes seemed to sear into her.

She didn't know what he meant. She felt his words resonate in her, and the exquisite ache that followed in their wake made her despair of ever really leaving this man, ever really surviving him.

"I didn't mean to disturb you, Mr. Vila." But her

voice was a jagged rasp of sound, and it gave her away.
It told him everything, she was sure of it. Angry, exhausted tears flooded her eyes, shaming her as much
as they infuriated her. She blinked them back, glad for
the excuse to look away from him.

He reached over and touched her, his hand hard and
warm on her upper arm. Dru froze; afraid, suddenly,
to meet his gaze. Afraid he would see all of the confu-
sion and attraction and hurt she so desperately wanted
to hide. Instead, she pretended to be vastly interested
in her hair, of all things, in the ponytail she'd pulled
it into and then drawn to the side and over her shoulder. She ran her hands over it, nervously. But he only
moved his hand to wrap his fingers around the length
of it himself, pulling gently on the silken length, tilting
her head up to face him before letting go.

Something sharp and near enough to sweet pierced
through her then, taking her breath. Maybe this was
only a dream. Maybe this was nothing but another one
of those Cayo dreams she'd wake from in such a panic
in her tiny bedsit, gasping out loud while her body
ached, alone and frustrated and wild with so much
emotion she could never release.

But she knew better.

"Tell me," he said, his voice low and still so powerful, filling her up, making her resolve and determina-
tion feel far too flimsy, far too malleable. Making her
wish she could simply be angry with him, and stay that
way. "Why do you really want to leave me?"

He didn't throw it at her. He asked. That and the
damp night surrounding them made it different, somehow. Made her look at him as if here, in the deepest
part of the night, he might be close enough to the man

she'd believed him to be that she could actually tell him a part of the truth.

But she blinked again, and the heat in her eyes reminded her who he really was.

"Why are you so determined I should stay?" she asked quietly. "You think so little of me. You believe I am good for nothing but a position as your assistant forever."

His hard mouth moved, though it was not a smile. "There are those who would kill for that privilege."

He was so close, the sheer masculine poetry of his beautiful torso *right there* and seemingly impervious to the chill, and it was astonishingly hard for Dru to keep her attention where it belonged.

And the fact that she still couldn't control her response to him—that it was as powerful now as it had been all along, as it had been three years ago—made her shiver, as if her body could no longer pretend it was unaffected. How else would she destroy herself, she wondered then in a kind of anguish, before this was done? How else would she sacrifice what mattered to her, her very self, on the altar of this man?

"I assume it was a punishment?" She searched his face, her heart plummeting as she saw what she always saw and nothing more. That implacable ruthlessness of his, that fierce beauty. As unreachable as the stars above her, concealed tonight by the clouds.

He frowned. "Why would I punish you?"

She felt her brows rise in disbelief. "Cadiz. Of course."

He made an impatient noise.

"Surely we have enough to discuss without beckoning in every last ghost," he said, but there was that odd note in his voice again. As if he did not believe himself, either.

"Just the one ghost." Her eyes never left his. "It was one little kiss, didn't we agree? And yet you punished me for it."

"Don't be absurd."

"You punished me," she repeated, firmly, despite the scratchiness she could hear in her voice. "And you were the one who started it."

He had done more than start it. He had ignited them both, set them afire. He'd had his arm thrown around her, and she'd been pleasantly full of *tortitas de camarones* and *calamares en su tinta,* Spanish sherry, and the heady knowledge that after the two years she'd been working for him, Cayo had finally shown her that there was more to him than his ruthless demands, his take-no-prisoners style of doing business. She'd smelled the hint of his expensive scent, like leather and spice, felt the incredible, hard heat that emanated from his skin beneath his clothes, and the combination had made her light-headed. She'd felt for him, and that heartbreaking scene with his grandfather. She'd ached for what he'd been through, what it had done to him. He'd *talked* to her that night, really talked to her, as if they were both simply people. As if there was more to them than the roles they played, the duties they performed.

It had been magical.

And then Cayo had swung her around, backing her up against the nearest wall. She'd seemed to *explode* into him, as if she'd been waiting for exactly that moment. He'd muttered words she didn't understand and then his mouth had been on hers, as uncompromising as anything else he did. All of that fire, all of that need, had rolled through her like a tempest, and she'd lost herself. She'd lost her head. It had been slick and dizzy and terrifyingly right and she'd found herself wrapped around him, her legs around his hips as he pressed that marvelous body of his against hers, his mouth plundering hers, taking and taking and taking—

It kept her up at night. Still.

"There was no punishment." Cayo's low voice snapped Dru back into the present.

His clever eyes probed hers in the dark, as if he could see straight into her memory, as if he knew exactly what it did to her even at three year's distance. As if he felt the same heat, the same longing.

As if he, too, wished they hadn't been interrupted three years ago.

The laughing group of strangers further down the walkway had drawn near. He'd set her down on her feet, gently. Almost too gently. They'd stared at each other, both breathing hard, both dazed, before continuing on to their hotel, where they'd parted in the hall outside their rooms without a word.

And they'd never discussed it again.

"Then why...?"

He raked a hand through his hair. "I didn't want you to leave," he said, his voice gruff. "There was no hidden agenda. I told you, I don't like to share." He blew out a breath, and when he spoke again, it was with an edge. "You are an integral part of what I do. Surely you know it."

She shook her head, unable to process that. The layers of it. What she knew he meant and, harder to bear, what she so desperately wanted him to mean instead. He was talking about work, she reminded herself fiercely, even as he looked at her with that fire in his dark amber eyes. He was always talking about work. For Cayo, there was nothing else. Why couldn't she accept it?

It was too much. It hurt.

"What are you so afraid of?" she asked before she could think better of it. Before she could question whether she wanted to hear the answer. "Why can't you just admit what you did?"

He scowled at her, and she thought he might snap something back at her, but he didn't. For a moment he looked torn, almost tortured, however little sense that made. The city was so quiet around them, as if they were the only people alive in the world, and Dru found herself biting down on her lower lip as if that smallest hint of pain could keep her anchored—and keep her from saying the things she knew she shouldn't.

This time, when he reached for her, he used the back of his hand and brushed it with aching gentleness over her cheek, soft and impossibly light, sending the hint of fire searing through her like the faintest kiss, until Dru's next breath felt like a sob.

"You're cold," he said, again in that gruff voice. That stranger's voice that nevertheless made her feel weak.

And she was chilly, it was true. She was trembling slightly. Uncontrollably.

If he wanted to think that was the cold, she wouldn't argue.

"Get some sleep," he ordered her, his eyes too dark, his mouth too grim.

And when he left her there, shaky and on the verge of more tears she hardly understood, her mind spinning as wildly as it had so long ago in Cadiz, it almost felt as if she'd dreamed it, after all.

Almost.

CHAPTER FIVE

CAYO was in a foul temper. He sipped his espresso, as harsh and black as his current mood, and eyed Drusilla over the top of it when she appeared at breakfast the next morning.

He had spent what was left of the night chasing the ghosts of his past out of his head, and failing miserably. Now, in the bright morning light, the opulence of the suite's great room like a halo all around her, Drusilla looked her usual, sleekly professional self—and he found it profoundly irritating. Gone was the woman he'd been unable to keep from touching on the terrace in the dark, her hair out of that ubiquitous twist she favored and so soft across her shoulder, wrapped up like a sweet-smelling gift in silk and soft cashmere. Gone as if she had been no more than a particularly haunting dream.

And still, he wanted her. Then. Now. In whatever incarnation she happened to present him with.

"We are going to Bora Bora," Cayo announced without preamble. "Have the butler order you the appropriate wardrobe."

He might have panicked, he thought with something like black humor, if he knew how. If he'd ever experienced something this confounding before. As it was, he only watched her walk toward him, and told himself that the pounding desire that poured through him was nothing more than resentment. Lack of sleep. Anything but what he knew it was.

She paused before dropping gracefully into the seat opposite him at the small table near the windows where he'd taken his breakfast, and he saw a host of emotions he couldn't quite identify chase across her face in a single instant before she smoothed it out into her customary neutrality.

That annoyed him, too.

"Has something happened with the Vila Resort there which requires your personal attention?" she asked, her voice as calm and unruffled as the rest of her—as if last night she hadn't sounded so uneven, so breakable. As if she hadn't spoken to him the way she would to the architect of her despair. As if he hadn't touched her like that, as though she were fragile. Precious, even.

What are you so afraid of? he heard her ask again, and it made something inside him seem to tear itself in half.

"It is a part of the Vila Group," he replied, in a voice far short of civility. "It all requires my personal attention."

Her too-knowing gray eyes met his, held for a moment, then dropped to the tablet she'd placed on the table before her. She smiled when the hovering staff placed a large silver pot of tea before her, and waved away the offer of food. And for some reason, her silence felt like a rebuke.

"We leave tonight," he said, his tone still clipped, though markedly more polite than it had been. He didn't know why he was responding meekly instead of as he'd prefer, which involved hauling her up and into his arms and dealing with all of this sexual tension once and for all. No matter what she thought of him—or what he thought of himself, for that matter. "Consider it my gift to you for your years of service, if you must."

Something flared in her gaze again, then disappeared behind that smooth, calm wall of hers he found he liked less and less the longer he looked at it. He wondered if it was as hard for her to maintain that courteous, professional veneer as it was becoming for him to keep his hands off her.

He rather doubted it.

"Will this 'gift' count as part of my final two weeks?" she asked lightly, though when her gaze met his, it hinted of steel. "Because that's all the time you have left, Mr. Vila. No matter what you choose to do with it."

"You said it was where you wanted to go," he reminded her, furious—at her for not accepting what he was reluctant to admit was an olive branch, and at himself for offering it in the first place. But something in the way she'd looked at him last night had burrowed deep beneath his skin. He could feel it now, like an impossible itch.

"Yes," she agreed softly. "I want to go to Bora Bora." She raised one delicate shoulder and then let it fall. "I never said I wanted to go with you."

That sat there between them.

There was no reason at all, Cayo reasoned, that it should feel like a slap when he could see clearly that she was only being frank. He already knew what she thought of him. Hadn't she been at such great pains to make sure of it? No matter how different it might have

appeared in the dark last night? He shouldn't be surprised, if that was what this odd feeling was. He wasn't.

"Life," he said after a moment, his accent thicker
than it should have been, almost as if his temper was
high, which wasn't in the least bit rational, "is all about
compromise."

"Really?" she asked. Her eyes searched his, and
she looked somewhere between amused and genuinely
baffled, which somehow made it worse. "How would
you know?"

Cayo tossed back the rest of his espresso and decided he was tired, that was all. There was no deeper
reason for any of this. How could there be? He hadn't
slept. That was why his head was so muddled. Why he
could not seem to sort through his own thoughts, his
own motivations. Nor even his own reactions.

"I am finding it difficult to track all of your accu-
sations," he said after a moment, his tone dry. Almost
conversational. "You believe I am a sociopath, yet last
night you told me I am also afraid. Today I am unfamiliar with compromise. Before, I was Godzilla, was
I not?" He was fascinated by the color that rose in
her cheeks, and then equally intrigued by the way she
squared her shoulders, as if withstanding an attack.
"I believe I take your meaning, Miss Bennett. I am a
monster without equal."

Monster. It was only a word, he told himself then,
as it seemed to echo hard in him, recalling that white-
washed village high in the Spanish mountains, his
grandfather's harsh pleasure on his eighteenth birthday. *It is just a word. It means nothing.*

"You are a man who assumes that his will is suffi-
cient permission to do anything he likes," Drusilla said
slowly, as if she were considering each word carefully.

"There are no consequences for the things you do." She reached for her tea, and poured a stream of the hot liquid into the delicate cup before her. Her gaze flicked to his, then away. "It would never occur to you to care."

He wanted to touch her with a new kind of fury, so intense was his desire to feel her skin against his. To take that mouth of hers and learn it, own it, make it his. To follow her down onto the nearest flat surface and lose himself inside her, at last.

But he did nothing of the kind. He held on to his control by the faintest, thinnest thread. Again.

"Of course not," he said coldly, as if there was nothing steaming up the air between them, as if there were no tension at all, no desire, no *need*. He reached for the *Financial Times* folded beside his plate and told himself he was dismissing her as he'd always done before, without thought. Without a single care, as accused. "That's what I pay you for."

It was a remarkably long trip.

I didn't want you to leave, he'd said.

Dru couldn't stop replaying it in her head, again and again. She handled the packing, the delivery of appropriate clothes for Cayo from the Milan ateliers he preferred and her own hurried selections from La Rinascente, the city's premier department store hardly a stone's throw from the Duomo. She sent out a flurry of emails, made the day's series of phone calls, and carried out the usual duties of her job, accustomed as she was to performing it wherever she happened to find herself.

But she couldn't seem to get last night out of her mind. The chill of the air, the inky dark and his hand so soft against her cheek. That storm in his midnight gaze that had crashed through her, too. That still did. Why should a few quiet words and a couple of touches affect her so? Why should she feel as if everything was different, when nothing seemed to have changed at all?

They boarded one of Cayo's jets in Milan late that evening, and Dru made her way to her usual bed-chamber. She stretched out on the bed and dared not let herself succumb to the turmoil inside herself, not when there was still the rest of her two weeks to live through. She couldn't let herself crack so soon. She'd never survive.

When she woke hours later, they simply went to work as if they were in the Vila Group's London headquarters rather than on a plane headed across the planet. She sat right there at his side in the area set apart for business. She queued up his calls, handling the many details of each, presenting him with the necessary documents and background materials he needed, and reminding him of anything he might have forgot or overlooked as the calls wore on. She prepped the various people who rang in, alerting them to Cayo's shifting moods and often suggesting ways to combat them. Between calls, they discussed various strategies to employ or different approaches to take to tackle each new issue or person.

"I'm tired of his games," Cayo said of one mutinous board member at one point, raking his hands through his hair in agitation. "I want to end him."

"That's one approach." Dru removed a stack of documents from in front of him and replaced them with another, larger stack. "Another might be to simply work around him the way you did with the Argentina project last year. Isolate him. Who will he play his games with then?"

Cayo eyed her for a moment, an approving gleam in his dark gaze that should not have given her so much pleasure.

"Who indeed?" he asked softly.

Dru made sure his coffee was always hot and fixed to his taste, and insisted that he eat something substantial after a certain span of time, simply serving him a meal if he refused to step away from the work at hand. When his voice took on that particularly icy edge that boded only ill, she calmly suggested he repair to the master suite to either rest or work out his temper on the exercise equipment that flew with him everywhere. She was on top of their travel plans, too; making certain that there was not the smallest chance that Cayo Vila should find himself inconvenienced in any small way, no matter where he was in the world or what he had to do. All of which she'd done a million times before.

But it wasn't the same.

Something really had changed last night, and it permeated even their most simple exchanges. The very air between them seemed electric, charged. Her hand brushed his and they both froze. She looked up from her tablet to find him watching her, a brooding sort of expression in those dark eyes of his, the gold in them gleaming in a way she didn't recognize. But she *felt* it. In her breasts, deep in her belly. In her limbs that were too heavy today, her breath that she couldn't quite catch.

It made her wonder. It made her too hot, too shivery, *too aware*. It made her want—again, anew—what she could never have.

Some seventeen hours into the almost twenty-four-hour trip, plus refueling stops, and they had worked roughly nine of them. Hardly half a day's work in Cayo's book, Dru knew. They took a break, sitting in the common area of the plane. Dru sipped at her water and knew better than to ask why Cayo was watching her with that new, disconcerting light in his eyes. Dark and considering, as if he had never seen her before. As if that strange, dream-like conversation on the terrace in Milan really had shifted something fundamental between them. That, she was sure, was why she felt almost watery, insubstantial. Needy and breathless. Unable to think about anything but Cayo, in all the ways she shouldn't.

"Why Bora Bora?" he asked. "When I suggested you take a holiday, I assumed you'd go to Spain. Portugal, perhaps. This seems like something of a reach."

Dru rolled the water bottle between her palms, letting the cold glass soothe her, letting the sound of the engines wash over her like white noise.

"Why *not* Bora Bora?" she asked lightly. "If working for you has taught me nothing else, it's to demand the best in all things."

"Indeed." Some fire flared there, in that golden topaz gaze, and for a moment she couldn't look away. Then his lips quirked into a hard sort of smile, sardonic and faintly amused. "I'm delighted to discover you take indolence as seriously as you take everything else."

"Perhaps all I want from life is to sit under a palm tree and stare at the sea," she said, though the very thought was faintly unnerving, somehow.

"And be waited upon hand and foot?" he asked, a note in his voice she couldn't decipher.

She thought of Dominic's ashes, packed away in the tin that functioned as an urn and sat in the center of her bookshelf back in London. And of the promises she'd made, to him and to herself. That she would let him go into the wind, the water. The least she could do was honor the man he might have been, had he made different choices, or been stronger against his own demons. And she knew that she needed it, too. The closure. The ceremony. A way to let go, once and for all.

"Something like that," she said now, not quite meeting Cayo's eyes.

He didn't believe her. She could see it in the way he shifted in his deep leather seat, as he scraped that thick, black hair back from his brow.

"How debaucherous." It was a taunt. And it hit hard, though she should have been impervious to him.

"I leave that kind of thing to you, Mr. Vila," she snapped.

Unwisely.

Everything seemed to pull taut. There was no air, no sound. Dru had the panicked sense that the plane had dropped from the sky—but no, Cayo did not move a muscle, it was only in her head. She felt her heart thud hard against her chest, then slow, and she could not seem to look away from him, from that hard mouth of his that she could not pretend she didn't crave. From that dangerous light in his eyes as he stared back at her.

"Is that a challenge, Miss Bennett?" he asked softly, that voice rolling through her, turning all of that need into an ache, insistent and sweet, burning her from the inside out. His cruel mouth moved into a hard smile, and she felt it like a caress. "I will endeavor to live up to your fantasies."

Did he know? Dru felt herself flush. Did he know what kept her awake—what tormented her, what she could see all too clearly even now—that delicious fusion of what had happened in Cadiz and on the yacht and what she imagined came next—

"But first," he continued in that silky, supremely dangerous tone, his gaze narrow on hers even as he gestured toward his phone again, "let's close this deal in Taiwan."

Dru felt hollowed out and more than a little light-headed with jet lag, not to mention her own much too vivid imagination, when they finally made it to what she assumed was Bora Bora, but which could have been anywhere for all she was able to discern in the thick, heavy dark.

The helicopter they'd taken after their landing in Tahiti set down in a small field lit with tall tiki torches. The night was close and warm, sultry against her skin. She could smell the sea and the deep green of wild, fragrant growing things. The sweetness of flowers hung heavy, like perfume against the dark, and when she tipped her head back to watch the helicopter fly away again, she had to stifle a gasp at the brilliance of the stars that crowded the night sky. The roar of the helicopter faded, leaving only a deep tropical hush behind. It seemed to arrow into her soul.

"Come," Cayo ordered her impatiently, and strode off.

Porters appeared from the darkness to handle the bags, and Dru followed Cayo over a wooden walkway, lit with more torches and hemmed in on all sides with lush greenery. Even in the dark, Dru could all but taste the burst of *jungle* all around her. Cayo was ahead of her, his long legs eating up the distance and before she knew it, she was hurrying—matching her stride to his, just as she'd always done.

Just like the dog on a leash he'd threatened to make

her, a small voice inside of her pointed out. She shook it off.

Cayo stopped walking before a large Polynesian-style house with high, arched rooftops and wide, open windows that stretched the length and width of the walls, featuring pulled-back sliding shutters and unobstructed views.

And on the other side of the walkway was water. Nothing but dark water, lapping gently against the shore, and off in the distance, a smattering of low lights. Dawn was coming, bluing the inky night. Dru could make out a mountain in front of her, off on its own island across the water, black and high.

"This is the villa," Cayo said.

He looked down at her as she drew closer to him, his ruthless face softened, somehow, by the soft tropical dark. Or perhaps she was only being fanciful. The torch lights surrounded them in a halo of golden light, and somehow made it seem as if they were standing even closer together than they were. As if there was nothing else in the world but the two of them, adrift in all this lushness.

"I don't know why you would ever leave a place like this," she said, trying to shift the focus back to the place. Away from the two of them. She smiled, but suspected it looked as nervous, as unsettled, as she felt. Still, she pushed on. "But perhaps it takes a different kind of imagination to conquer the world from this far-off little corner of it."

And suddenly he was too close, though she hadn't seen him move. He loomed above her, his shoulders wider than they should have been and his chest too broad, and he was too close for Dru to breathe, too close for her to do anything but lose herself in the dangerous amber of his gaze.

Her pulse went crazy beneath her skin. Her mouth went dry. And she felt that long, low ache between her legs.

His hard gaze slammed into hers, as if he meant to hold her there with the force of it. And sure enough, Dru found she couldn't move.

"Don't speak to me like I'm another one of those investors," he said fiercely. Almost angrily. "Don't expect me to dance to your tune simply because you make a bit of cocktail conversation."

He was right, she had been doing exactly that—and she hated that he'd seen it so clearly. That he'd seen *her*. She'd always thought she'd wanted that but the truth of it terrified her. It was her job to read him, not the other way around. Never the other way around!

"My apologies," she bit out. "I won't point out your lack of imagination again."

He didn't speak. He only reached over and dragged his thumb across her lips, testing their shape, and it wasn't a soft touch, a lover's caress. It was starkly, undeniably sexual. If she hadn't known better, if it hadn't been impossible and unthinkable, Dru would have said he was staking his claim. Imprinting her with his touch, as he might brand cattle or stamp a logo onto a product. Leaving his mark.

She should have slapped his hand away. Instead, she burned. Long and slow and deep.

The way she always had. The way she always would.

"Believe me," he said, and his voice was so soft and still so demanding. So consuming. A thread of sound in the sultry night, surrounded by flickering golden light and the wild, incapacitating staccato of her own heartbeat. "My imagination grows more vivid by the hour."

Dru's lips felt as if they were on fire, and she could feel his touch all through her body, coursing through her veins, even after he dropped his hand and eased away. Her heart didn't stop its frantic beating. Her mouth was still so dry, her stomach in a knot. She felt him everywhere. And for a long moment, he only looked at her, his dark eyes hot and shrewd and that cruel mouth impassive.

And even that felt like a touch, and with the same result.

Cayo turned then to greet the smiling man who approached them, from inside the villa Dru realized she'd forgot about entirely. When he looked back at her, his gaze was too dark to read.

I didn't want you to leave, he'd said on the terrace in Milan, half a world away now. And still it rang in her, through her, like a bell. *I still don't.*

She wanted that to mean something. She *wanted.* And she could still feel his touch moving through her, making her his as surely as if he'd tattooed his name on her skin in the blackest ink.

You're tired and overwrought, she told herself, fighting back another surge of heat behind her eyes. *Nothing will feel like this in the morning. It can't.*

"You look exhausted," Cayo said, his gaze moving over her face, making her imagine he could read her every thought that easily. He nodded, as if coming to some kind of decision, and the way his mouth curved then looked self-mocking. "Frederic will show you to your rooms."

And then he walked away, disappearing into the thick night.

Leaving her to make sense of what was happening to her—to them—on her own.

Fighting off emotions she couldn't understand, much less process, Dru obediently followed Frederic through the villa. There were tall, vaulted ceilings and the same rich, dark wood she'd seen outside. Airy, spacious rooms without proper windows, simply cut-out spaces in the walls to let in paradise on all sides. Bright-colored wall hangings, low and inviting sofas in magentas and creams. Polynesian artifacts on built-in shelves in the walls, and glorious flowers scattered across ornamental tables. She followed Frederic down a level and then outside again. They walked along another, far shorter path that delivered her to a private bungalow splayed out over its own private pier. Here, too, the walls were open to the night, letting the softest of breezes into the expansive suite. Dru couldn't seem to breathe deeply enough to take it all in.

And again—still—all she wanted to do was dissolve into the tears she knew were waiting for her and cry herself dry. Cry until she couldn't feel this anymore, whatever this was: Cayo and the dark and that touch, imprinted on her skin. Claiming her.

With a smile, Frederic showed her the glass floor hidden away beneath a rug in the sitting area.

"In the day," he promised, "you will see many fish. Even turtles."

"Thank you," she whispered, summoning her smile from somewhere.

"Sleep now," the man said kindly. "It will be better when you sleep."

And she wanted to believe him. She did.

Everything felt too huge, too unwieldy, she thought when he left. Her own head. This place. Cayo, of course. Cayo most of all. It all felt impossible, and painful. It hurt from the inside out. She moved over to the opening across from the four-poster bed draped in filmy mosquito netting from high above, and looked out at the water and the smudge of orange light behind the mountain in the distance. Daybreak was coming. And she was in paradise with the devil, and she burned for him as if she'd already fallen. Perhaps she had. Perhaps that was why this had hurt so much from the start.

There was no reason at all she should cry now. She wiped away the tear that tracked its way down her cheek. And then all the ones that followed. She felt her face crumple in on itself, and had to pull on reserves she hadn't known she had to breathe through it—to fight back the sobs that she knew lurked *just there* and would be the end of her.

She must not give in. *She must not start.* It was only two weeks, and less than that now. She needed to be strong only a little while longer.

Oh, Dominic, she thought as she crawled on to the bed, not even bothering to change out of the clothes she'd been wearing across several continents and more time zones than she could count. *I wish you could see this place. It's even better than you dreamed.*

Her last thought as she drifted off into blessed unconsciousness was of Cayo. That mesmerizing curve of his hard, impossible mouth. The touch of his hand in the cold, wet dark, so hot against her chilled skin. That unquenchable fire that burned ever hotter, ever brighter by the day, no matter how she tried to deny it. No matter how hard she fought. He would destroy her. She knew it. She'd always known it—it was one of the foremost reasons she had to leave him.

So there was no reason at all that she should be smiling against the soft white pillows as she drifted off into oblivion.

CHAPTER SIX

DRU woke to sunshine on all sides. It streamed in the open windows of her room, bathing her in light and the sweet, fragrant breeze. It felt like some kind of blessing, chasing away what shadows remained from the long night before. She stretched luxuriously on the soft mattress and told herself she was fine now. Fully restored. Cayo's touch, his talk of debauchery, that fire that only seemed to build between them—it was all part of a darkness dispelled. She was sure of it.

She rose from her bed and dressed slowly, in deference to the sultry weather. She pulled on a loose and flowing pair of linen trousers and paired them with a strappy black vest. Then she swept all of her hair up into as sleek a ponytail as was possible in this climate. The result, she thought, frowning at herself in the mirror, was as close to tropical and yet professional as she was likely to get. She slipped on a pair of thonged sandals and stepped outside, where it appeared to be well into a perfect afternoon.

Dru blinked in the brightness and took in her surroundings. There was another pier down from her bungalow with a selection of small watercraft drawn up to it and on the shore nearby. She could see water in all directions, a darker blue on the far side of the island

and that stunning turquoise beneath her bungalow in what must be the famous Bora Bora Lagoon.

She walked back into the villa and was struck anew by the beauty she'd only partially registered last night. The dark wood, the high ceilings to draw up the day's heat, all of it exposed to the tropical paradise and thus a part of it, too. The jungle pressed in on all sides, with the sea just beyond. It felt as wild as it did welcoming, and made something in her seem to ease as she stood there.

When she finished eating a simple meal of toast and tea out on one of the many terraces overlooking the water, she felt restless. Cayo typically did not expect her to rush to work after a long-haul flight unless he had explicitly stated otherwise, so she didn't feel she had to seek him out at once. She assured herself any employee would feel the same—that it had nothing to do with all the churning emotion he'd stirred in her the night before. *Nothing at all.* Instead, she wandered down to the wooden path and followed it. It ran down to the pier, then on, making its lazy way down to the farthest point of the island and then looping back around.

Palm trees rustled over her head and bright flowers bloomed jubilantly on either side of the tidy boardwalk. She could hear birds up above and the waves against the shore. It made perfect sense to her that Dominic would have wanted this to be his final resting place. The sun was warm on her face, the breeze a caress against her skin. She felt serene. At peace.

All you needed was a good night's sleep, she told herself firmly.

As the villa came into view again, perched up over its own gleaming white beach, she saw there was a whole section of it she'd yet to explore. It was not until she left the path and climbed up for a closer look that she realized that what looked like a separate wing was, in fact, Cayo's master suite.

The wide-open walls meant she could step inside too easily and so, giving into an urge she didn't recognize, she stepped into the first of the rooms, and then sucked in a sharp breath. It was an airy space appointed with deft masculine touches, bold colors and clean lines, but the centerpiece was the massive bed that dominated the room. *Cayo slept here last night,* a little voice whispered. Or perhaps more recently, as it was still unmade, the snowy white coverlet tossed to one side, the pillows dented.

And suddenly, Dru went hot all over. Then cold. Almost as if she was feverish.

She reached over and traced the indentation in the nearest pillow with a fingertip. She imagined him naked and dark against the crisp sheets, that perfect, impossible body on display, her own body softening and melting at the pictures in her head—

It was clearly time to find the man—her boss, she reminded herself sharply—and concentrate on what remained of her time in this job, not on her incurable madness where he was concerned. Not on the way she burned.

She glanced at the art and small collections of statues and carvings as she made her way down the hall, peering into each room as she passed. There was a library fitted with a wall of books, a seating area within and a covered lanai outside with a plush loveseat and two armchairs—perfect for a read in the shade. There was a private lounge with a flat-screen television on one wall and a fire pit with a dramatic chimney on the other, and what looked like a built-in bar in the corner.

And then an office suite, kitted out with computers and other equipment, sleek modern furniture—and Cayo.

Dru stopped in the doorway, watching him as he frowned down at his laptop with his mobile clamped to his ear, as usual. His hair looked unruly, as if he'd spent hours raking it back with his fingers, and he'd neglected to shave. It made him look even more dark and sexy than usual. Unpredictable, somehow. Edgy.

"You misunderstand me," he was saying in cold, deadly French into his mobile. "It is no matter to me whether we ever open a plant in Singapore. But I suspect it is of great importance to you. Perhaps you'd like to rethink your tactics?"

He looked absurdly beautiful, as if someone had carved him into being from the finest stone and set him among lesser statues. He fairly gleamed in the golden sunlight streaming in behind him. He looked terrible and great the way the old gods might have, dangerous and mighty, and if he'd announced that he could command the weather at his whim, she would have believed it. The storm within her howled into being anew, the fever and the yearning, and he was to blame.

He raised his head then and met her gaze. Her stomach dropped and she stopped kidding herself about *serenity* and *a good night's sleep*. It was as if he was inside her, provoking her, making her ache and burn.

He looked at her as if she were naked and beneath him. And Dru couldn't help but wish she was, no matter how much she hated herself for her own eternal weakness.

Cayo sat back in his chair, his eyes on her as he finished the call with an abruptness that she knew must have made the man on the other end wince. He tossed his mobile on to the desktop in front of him and then regarded her, his golden eyes narrow and much too shrewd. His olive skin seemed darker against the loose white shirt he wore, making it impossible not to notice his lean, muscled arms and that perfect chest. Her breasts swelled against her vest. Her palms felt damp. And there was that same familiar ache, blooming into life so low in her belly.

Sleep or no sleep, she was doomed.

"Henri is still giving you trouble?" she asked, determined to ignore what was happening to her, what she felt. Desperate to concentrate on business instead.

"He remains unclear on the chain of command," Cayo replied, though the way he looked at her made her think he was not thinking of Henri or the Singapore project at all. "I think he has already convinced himself that I am not, in fact, the majority shareholder now."

"You expected that," Dru reminded him. She reached out a hand and touched the door frame next to her, running her finger over the dark wooden beam. The slightly rough texture made her feel even warmer, somehow, as if she was touching him instead. "You felt his personal connection with the employees and his decades of company loyalty far outweighed any tussles over authority you might have to have."

"So I did." He leaned against the arm of his chair and propped up his jaw in his hand, eyeing her in a way that made her keenly aware that he was one of the most powerful men in the world and she was…the only person she knew who had tried to defy him. "How do you find Bora Bora? Is it living up to your expectations?"

Dru couldn't seem to hold his gaze for more than a second at a time, and had no idea why. She felt…fluttery. It was as if he really had branded her last night with that odd, small touch in the dark, and she didn't know how to regain her equilibrium. Not when he was in front of her like this. Her lips seemed to tingle all over again, as if remembering. *Yearning.*

"I don't understand you," she said.

"That is hardly a breaking news item," he said dryly. "What is it you feel you need to understand? I am a simple man, when all is said and done. I like what I like." His hard mouth curved, his dark eyes gleamed gold. "I want what I want."

She ignored the way his voice lowered so suggestively, the images that it conjured before her and the wildfires it sent spinning over her skin. She dropped her hand to her side and nodded at the view behind him. An infinity pool lay on the far side of the patio, the water as smooth as glass, surrounded by more of the smooth dark wood, and beyond it, the endless sea. Yet Cayo sat with his back to it, more interested in his laptop computer, the documents spread out before him on the desk, the television on the wall tuned, as ever, to the financial news.

"You haven't been here in years." She knew she should walk to the desk, sit down, act appropriately and do her job, but she couldn't bring herself to move that close to him. Not so soon after the last two nights of all that savage intensity. Not yet. "Not in as long as I've worked for you."

"It was eight years ago, I believe," he agreed, that lean body much too still, as if he was deliberately leashing all of his power as he sat and watched her. As he *waited.* "When I bought the place from some Saudi prince or another."

Dru bit at her lip, that fluttery feeling twisting and suddenly too close to another surge of what felt like tears. As if it was impossible to be around him without all of this emotion welling up in her. She was afraid she might simply burst.

"I don't understand the point of owning beautiful things you never see." Her voice should have sounded casual. Easy. Not...raw. Wounded. She was supposed to be so good at this kind of thing! "And now that you're here for the first time in almost a decade, you're sitting inside in an office, working. Moving all your money and power about like an endless game of chess. Why bother collecting all these little pieces of paradise if you never plan to let yourself enjoy them?"

He looked at her for a beat, then another. And then that same look she'd seen the night before, as if he'd come to some kind of decision, gleamed in his eyes. A little chill snaked down Dru's back. Cayo moved from his chair, rising to his feet and prowling toward her.

Dru had to fight to stand still—not to break and run. He stopped when he was a foot or so away, and that cruel mouth of his, brutally sensual and entirely too dangerous, quirked slightly in the corner. Dru felt it like another touch, like the hand he'd pressed against her cheek in Milan, like his thumb across her mouth last night. Her blood seemed too hot in her veins, her skin felt too tight across her body, and when she reached over to grab the doorjamb again, it was because her legs were too weak to hold her upright.

And still, he only looked at her. Through her. Making the fire inside her leap high, burn white.

"I appreciate your concern," he said in that silky voice that teased along her oversensitive skin, moved like a shiver down her spine, and then made even her bones ache. "It's too bad you insist upon leaving me. We could play chess with my properties together."

"What a lovely idea," she said with a great insincerity she took no pains to conceal, and which made him look something close enough to amused. "But I am terrible at chess."

"I find that hard to believe." She thought he nearly smiled then, gazing down at her. "You are always at least six moves ahead. You'd excel at it."

She had the oddest sense of déjà vu for a moment and then it came to her—he was talking to her like a person. Not as his employee, but as another human being. Someone he actually knew. The last time he'd done this, he'd teased her in just this way. They'd smiled. They'd told stories, shared parts of themselves over small dishes of food and large glasses of wine. Or she'd thought they had. That had been that long dinner in Cadiz, before their fateful walk home, and Dru couldn't stand her own treacherous heart, the way it softened for him anew, as if she didn't know exactly where moments like this led. Precisely nowhere, with a three-year detour through infatuated subservience.

She could not let him reel her in. Not again.

"I'm not here to play games," she said quietly, hoping he couldn't hear the unevenness in her voice, that clash between what was good for her and what she wanted. "I'm here to be your personal assistant. The only other offer on the table was to be your dog. On a leash. Isn't that what you said? Is that what you'd prefer?"

His gaze heated, becoming so molten she could hardly bear it, though she didn't look away. His mouth twisted. She remembered belatedly that he was much too close, his potent masculinity and all of that restless, brilliant power of his bright and brilliant between them, making her swallow hard. Making her feel too hot, too weak, all at once.

"If you want to be my pet you must sit," he growled at her. Daring her. Commanding her. "Stay. *Surrender.*"

And the worst part was, she very nearly obeyed.

"I do appreciate the offer," Dru whispered when she could speak, but she hardly heard her own voice, lost as it was in the thunder of her heartbeat, the shriek and clamor of the storm only gaining strength inside her. "But I think I'll pass."

She should have moved—but she didn't. She only stood there, paralyzed, as Cayo closed the distance between them and stretched an arm up, over his head, to brace himself against the doorjamb and look down directly into her face.

She thought of old gods again, stunning and un-predictable, implacable and fierce. Something deep inside her seemed to go very, very still. He leaned there, propped up in the doorway, dark eyes and that sinful body, exuding the ruthlessness and command that made him who he was.

Worse than that, he looked at her as if he knew her at least as well as she knew him. As if he could read her as easily as she'd learned to read him. And the very notion was as terrifying—as impossible—as it had been before.

"Tell me," he said, his voice even lower, his golden amber eyes so hot she worried they might blister her skin or consume her whole. "What are *you* hiding from?"

For a moment, she looked almost as if he'd punched her in the stomach. But then she blinked, the mask Cayo had come to hate descended, and she even produced a strained sort of smile.

That might have irritated him, but he was done with

this. He'd decided he would have her no matter what games she played, and he would lick that wall away if he had to. He looked forward to it.

"The only thing I've been hiding from today is our workload," she said brightly. Hiding, he knew. Right there in front of him. "Perhaps we should get to it."

"Forget about work," he growled, a sentence that had never crossed his lips before, perhaps not ever. And he didn't allow himself to consider the ramifications of that—all he could seem to concentrate on was the confusing woman in front of him. And how very much he wanted her, despite all the reasons he knew that was a bad idea. "We're in Bora Bora. Work can wait."

"I beg your pardon?" She looked unduly horrified.

"What's the point of being the boss if I can't decree a holiday on a whim?" he asked, striving for a lighter tone and, if that look on her face was any indication, failing. "Didn't you suggest I enjoy myself in paradise not five minutes ago?"

"To hell with the consequences, is that it?" she asked, throwing that back at him, and her eyes flashed as if she was angry with him. Which grated.

He didn't understand any of this. He didn't understand what was happening to him, and he certainly didn't understand why everything he said made her so unhappy, or so furious. Or both at once. Why she leaped from boats to escape him, then looked at him on a dark Italian terrace with all the world in her eyes and spoke of *punishment,* making him feel small three years later.

He was not a man who dealt well in uncertainties.

But what he did know was passion. Sex and desire. He had built his life around what he wanted. He knew *want.* And much as she claimed to hate him, much as she threw words or shoes at his head, he knew she wanted him as much as he wanted her. He could see it. He'd always seen it, if he was honest with himself. And he was tired of fighting off the only thing that made sense in all of this.

"Consequences are for lesser men," he said.

He'd already decided. When he'd walked away from her last night despite the way he burned to take her, when he'd found himself handling his own brutal need alone in his shower, he'd known he was done with this. She was leaving him anyway. There was only so much complication that could occur in the time she had left. Why was he denying himself? He was not the kind of man who did without the things he wanted.

She blinked at his arrogance, but that was better. He didn't want the threat of tears, the sting of her temper. And he certainly didn't want that neutral wall of hers, designed to keep the world at an icy remove. He wanted heat. He wanted that fire again, and who cared anymore what burned?

"Come," he said. It was an order. He didn't pretend otherwise. "Kiss me."

Drusilla's eyes flew wide. One hand went to her throat. He imagined he could feel her pulse there, imagined it kicking against his own hand instead of hers. He wanted to press his mouth to her skin and taste her excitement for himself.

"What did you say?" Her voice was no more than a whisper.

"You heard me."

"I am not going to kiss you," she said, coming over all flustered and something like prim then, her gray eyes brimming with outrage.

Yet behind it, mixed in with it, that consuming, dis-

tracting heat that matched his. That called to him. That
meant, he knew, that he already had her. It was only
a matter of time.

"But you will, Drusilla," he promised her. "Trust me."

Dru didn't know why she wasn't running away from
him.

Her heart pounded so hard it made her feel faint,
everything inside her seemed to be in revolt, and yet
she only stood there. Gazing back at him, while un-
certainty and longing howled and fought and pooled
between her legs in a hot pulse of desire.

"Don't call me that," she said instead of all the other
things she could have said—*should* have said. What
was the matter with her? Why couldn't she seem to
summon the will to protect herself the way she should?

"Your name?" His eyes gleamed like gold. He was
so close, so arrogant and sure, and it was harder and
harder to remember all the reasons she shouldn't let
herself fall over this particular cliff. All the reasons
she shouldn't jump headfirst, for that matter.

"My mother is the only person who ever called me
Drusilla," she found herself telling him as if she were
not standing in this doorway torn apart by tension,
while her body clamored for things she was afraid to
look at too closely. And far more afraid to do. Or not
do. She wasn't sure which scared her more. "And I
have not laid eyes on that woman in at least ten years."

"Dru, then," he said, and it moved through her like
honey, her name in his mouth. It set fires in her in
places she hardly knew existed. It felt like a lock fall-
ing open, but she knew better than to give in to that.
She knew better than to trust herself around this man.

Look at what a kiss had wrought! "And I think you want to be on my leash, after all. Don't you?"

There was no denying the sensual intent behind that question. Or the frank appraisal in his eyes.

Or what it did to her.

The hall fell away. The world with it. There was only him. Only Cayo. Nothing but the exquisite tautness that wound around them, stealing her breath, making his eyes seem to glow. There were scarcely two feet between them and yet all she could focus on was his mouth and that carnal knowledge, that masculine certainty, in the way he looked at her.

She should have said something. Anything.

When she only gazed at him, fighting for breath, unable to speak, his eyes went dark with a need she was afraid she recognized all too well.

"Then come." Another order, which should have enraged her. His mouth curved into something sardonic—and impossibly sexy. Those wicked brows rose in challenge. "Heel."

She felt the words sizzle through her, white-hot and life-altering, and that was when she knew with a sharp burst of clarity that there was only one way this would end. She knew him, didn't she? Cayo's attention span when it came to the women who shared his bed was famously short. If she really wanted to leave him, if she really wanted to be free of this hold he seemed to have on her, then this was the way to do it. This was a one-way street. No turning back.

No matter what it cost her.

"Well?" he asked softly, taunting her.

Dru swallowed, hard. She held his gaze for a long moment, understanding that this was a line she could never uncross. That she had no idea, really, what giving in to this kind of inferno might do to her—the damage it might cause. She'd spent three years recovering from a kiss, after all. She couldn't imagine what this would do.

But it didn't matter now. He looked at her with that certainty in his eyes, that sheer male confidence and stark carnal promise, and she knew that she didn't have it in her to walk away from this. Not when she'd spent so long imagining it, fantasizing about it. Yearning for it with everything she had.

Who cares how you have him, so long as you do? a greedy voice inside her asked, and she didn't have it in her to disagree. She'd lost her will to fight somewhere high above the Pacific Ocean. She didn't have to lose herself, too. She wouldn't, she promised herself. This was a strategy, not a surrender.

She closed the distance between them, watching the light in his fascinating eyes burn ever brighter the closer she came. She slid her hands over the taut planes of his chest, reveling in his heat, his bold strength. There was no going back—but there was no way forward, either, without this. And the truth was that she wanted him. She always had. This way she could have everything—she could have Cayo in the way she'd dreamed of since Cadiz, and then her freedom in a little over a week. In every way that mattered, this was a victory.

It was, she assured herself, her gaze searching his. *It was.* But what she felt was that wild flame searing into her, burning through her, making all these things she clung to, all these things she told herself, so much ash.

"Please do not tell me that you intend to do all of this in tedious slow motion," Cayo said, that curve in his mouth telling her he was teasing her again and connecting hard to all the places that longed for him like this, for his touch, turning her fever for him ever higher. "I believe that is far more entertaining in films than in real life."

"For God's sake," she said, no longer his assistant, not in a moment like this. Not when they were changing everything, no doubt for the worse, and she couldn't even pretend to care about that as she should. "Shut up."

And then Dru stretched up onto her toes, plastered herself against the length of him, and doomed herself forever by pressing her mouth to his.

CHAPTER SEVEN

SHE tasted the way he remembered. Better. So hot and good and *his*.

Cayo's arms came around her, pulling her against him, into him, needing to feel the weight of her breasts against his chest, the softness of her belly against the thrust of his hardness, the gentle swell of her hips against his. He kissed her again and again, reveling in the punch of it. The kick.

And she met him. Her arms wrapped around his neck, her mouth moved against his with the same urgency, the same demand. He thought she said his name. He wasn't sure he could speak or if he did, what language he might use, or if it would all come out as nonsense. He didn't care.

She was intoxicating, and he could finally let himself indulge in her as he wished.

At last, he sank his hands into her dark hair, exulting in the feel of it, the scent. Warm silk and the faint hint of vanilla. He pulled out the band that held her hair and let the mass of waves fall around her shoulders. He angled his mouth for a better fit, gathering her closer, taking what he wanted, at last.

He smoothed his hands down the sensual curve of her back, then tested her pert bottom, making them both groan when he moved her against the thrust of his arousal. It wasn't enough. It was barely a start. He took and he took until she was gasping his name, breathing hard, and he had to rein himself in. Or have her right there in the hallway—and he had no intention of going too quickly.

Not with this woman. Not with Dru. Not when it felt as if he'd waited lifetimes for this. For her.

He moved to taste, briefly, the freckles the sun had already raised across the bridge of her nose, then traced the line of her cheekbone, her satiny cheek, her stubborn jaw. She smelled of coconut and flowers, and tasted like magic, and he could not seem to get close enough.

She made a small noise in the back of her throat, like a purr, and it nearly undid him. *Mine,* he thought, with a surge of possessive triumph. *All mine.*

He took her hand in his, marveling at how delicate she was, how perfectly formed. He led her down the hall, the afternoon sun still golden and shining through the windows of the rooms they passed, and he couldn't pretend he didn't feel victory thump through him like a drumbeat when she simply followed him like this, those gray eyes dizzy with want—very much like the docile, biddable female she had pretended to be for so many years, but wasn't. The surrender of a strong woman, he thought with pure male satisfaction, was so much more exciting than that of a weak one. He intended to revel in hers.

Once in his bedroom, he pulled her to him again, luxuriating in the feel of her in his arms. *Finally.*

He took her mouth again, kissing her anew as he maneuvered her toward the bed. When the back of her knees hit the mattress she pulled away and looked up at him, her breath coming too fast, her fathomless gray eyes dark now and dazed with need, her pretty face soft and flushed and *his*.

She was his.

Cayo didn't speak. He didn't counter his own uncharacteristic possessiveness, or even try. Nothing about Dru had made sense so far, not since that rainy morning in London when she'd changed everything he took for granted. Why should this? He tugged the vest up over her head, sliding it over all of that long, dark hair, and smiled when he saw her royal blue bra and the round breasts he'd only glimpsed through her wet blouse before now.

"Perfecto," he murmured, and leaned down to press his mouth against the crest of one breast, sucking on it through the thin, glossy material. Dru gasped, and so he did the same with the other, waiting until her head was thrown back and her eyes closed before he reached around and unhooked the bra. She reached to pull it from her arms and he bent and licked the closest nipple, pulling it into his mouth.

And Dru went wild.

Cayo got lost in it then, in her. In her heat, her softness, her beautiful cries. He stripped her trousers from her long, sleek legs, then that other scrap of satin and lace. He hardly noticed as he shrugged out of his own clothes, because it wasn't fast enough, it meant he wasn't touching her, and it took entirely too long before he was naked and she was sprawled across his bed the way he wanted her, the way he'd wanted her for longer than he'd been aware of it. This was no new need that roared in him, demanding he take her again and again until they were both sated. What moved in him felt old and complicated, as if he'd hidden it from himself. But he wasn't hiding any longer. He stretched out beside her, propping himself up on one arm, fiercely satisfied to see her nipples were hard and her tattletale English skin was pink and rosy.

His.

She rolled as if she meant to begin exploring him herself, but he pressed her back down.

"But I want—"

"Sit," he murmured, tracing a finger down to her breast and toying with its peak, making Dru arch from the bed with a moan.

He bent to replace his fingers with his lips, and she cried out again, writhing beneath him as he tugged her nipple into the heat of his mouth even as he cupped her other breast in his hand. Then he kissed his way down the gentle swell of her abdomen, licking over her navel and the gentle curve of her hips. He learned she had a trio of small birthmarks near her left hip bone, and that she couldn't keep her hips still, especially when he held them between his hands and then curved his fingers around to test the shape and sweet, silken perfection of her bottom.

And then he parted her thighs and kissed his way even lower.

"Cayo—" she started again, naked passion in that voice, so full of *want* it made his hardness ache in response.

"Stay," he ordered her, and licked his way into her molten core, exulting in the fresh, hot taste of her desire.

She arched from the bed again, her hips rising to meet his mouth as he took her, tasted her, made her his. Unequivocally. And then she exploded all around him, sobbing out his name as she fell off the side of the world.

And it was not nearly enough.

He moved back up the bed, and pulled her to him, then rolled them both, sitting up and lifting her so she sat astride him. He wanted to see her. He wanted to see everything.

"Cayo…" She whispered his name, her eyes fluttering open, to gaze at him as he pressed against the core of her.

She was wet and hot and soft, and he wanted her so badly he nearly shook with it. He held her bottom in his hands, lifted her, and watched as she shivered in turn when he slid himself along the entrance to her core, teasing her. Her gray eyes darkened again. She pulled her perfect lower lip between her teeth. She lifted her arms and wrapped them around his shoulders, bringing her breasts flush against his chest.

"Surrender," he whispered, and then he drove into her, and there was nothing at all but fire.

That perfect, encompassing fire. It roared through him, into him. It incinerated everything he thought, everything he knew, until there was nothing at all but Dru. And she was supple and curvy and draped all around him. She began to move her hips and he groaned, too close to the edge.

He wrapped his hands around her hips to slow her down, then set his own pace. Slow. Deliberate. Torturing them both. Hot and endless strokes that made him grit his teeth and made her drop her head to his neck and sob out her pleasure. He moved her up and down as he thrust into her, again and again, wanting it never to end. Wanting to stay balanced in all this lush perfection forever. Wanting to breathe her in like this, so deep inside her he hardly knew which one of them was which.

She lifted her head then and her gaze locked with his. Held. He felt her breath on his face, her legs tight around him, and still he moved, building that fire into a raging blaze, making her moan even louder, watching those gray eyes of hers glaze over with the same incomparable passion that stormed through him. Taking him over. Making him want nothing more than to burn in it, over and over, too hot to bear, until there was nothing left of him.

This is Dru, he thought, unable to stop looking at her, touching her, feeling her in every part of him. *And this is mine.*

And he understood then that he had no intention of ever letting her go. Whatever that might mean.

She closed her eyes and threw back her head, her lovely back arching toward the setting sun through the windows behind her, the fading light casting her lush body in oranges and golds.

Like some kind of pagan goddess, and all of her his.

She started to shudder again, wild and untamed in his arms, and when she called out his name this time, he followed her over the edge. At last.

Dru lay tangled with him in the wide bed and watched the sun drip down toward the sea, then melt away.

She could not seem to form coherent thoughts. There was only the buzzing in her limbs and under her skin, like some kind of high-voltage live wire, still sending out sparks. She felt Cayo's hard shoulder beneath her cheek. She felt the heat of his skin and the way his chest rose and fell. She did not think. She wasn't sure she wanted to think. She watched the sky instead.

Cayo stirred beside her when the sun dropped below the horizon, as if roused by the twilight. He turned to face her, his eyes dark and once again unreadable in the deep shadows of his chamber.

He slid his hand up to hold her cheek and then brought her face to his. For a moment he only gazed at her, and she felt a great stillness inside her, a kind of hush. As if she was waiting for something, poised on the edge of another high cliff while all the rest of her seemed to shiver.

The clock is already ticking, a voice whispered inside her head, ruthlessly practical when Dru felt anything but. *He's already gone.*

But as if he could hear her, he kissed her. Deep and slow. Sweet. Addicting. And then the fire kicked in. As if it could never be quenched. As if none of this would ever be enough. She had been a terrible fool, she acknowledged as his hand moved over her face, angling her mouth closer to his for a better fit, a deeper kick. She should have known better than to think she could handle this. She would leave him as planned, she understood then in some deep, primitive way, but then she would mourn him, and she might never stop. She had walked right into this, and there was nothing for her but Miss Havisham and regret on the other side of it. And still she kissed him, unable to help herself. Unable to stop what she'd already started, what she'd already done.

No sense borrowing trouble, she thought then, in some desperation. It would come no matter what she did. It would hurt. Maybe she'd always known that.

He rose over her in the bed and settled himself between her legs, and Dru let go of a future that seemed far away from this moment, too far away to matter. He settled his weight on his hands and looked down at her, still watching her with those too-shrewd eyes of his.

"Dru," he said. Just her name. As if he was tasting it.

"Cayo," she replied in kind, feeling far too vulnerable. She didn't know what he saw when he looked down at her like that. She didn't know how to prevent him from seeing everything, all of her hopes and fears and terrors, not when she had abandoned herself so completely to be with him like this.

But he simply twisted his hips and thrust into her. Slick. Hot.

And she stopped caring what he saw. What he knew. She concentrated instead on the sleek perfection of this age old dance between them. As if she'd been made to fit him, just like this.

He moved slowly, hypnotically. As if he did not wish to build that fire between them this time so much as encourage it to burn high on its own. She matched his lazy rhythm, her hips rising to meet his, every part of her exulting in the way they fit together. In the way they moved together. Slow and easy and devastating.

She told herself it was the only thing that mattered.

This time, she could reach up and explore the sheer beauty of his lean, smooth torso. She ran her hands over his hard pectorals, then trailed her way down that mouthwatering abdomen. Smooth skin stretched across steel. Hard male beauty unlike any other. Ferocious and proud. Fierce and demanding. She pulled herself up from the bed to kiss his chest, to taste the bold heat of him, the incomparable strength. The delectable power.

The pace began to change, then, the fire burning ever hotter. Cayo's shoulders blocked out the world, and she forgot everything but this. Everything but him. Everything but the wildness they made here, and the way it stormed through her, tearing her apart from within.

He slid down to pull her close and she loved it. The full, hard weight of him against her, pressing her into the bed, making her feel somehow small and yet cherished, all at once. She could feel his breath in her ear, and then he began to murmur words she didn't know in Spanish, crooning against the length of her neck while still he thrust into her, over and over and over again. She wrapped her legs around his hips and clung to him, mindless and wanton, entirely at his command. And when he reached between them and pressed his fingers against the heart of her need, she burst into a million pieces. Again.

He kept on as she shattered around him, until he shouted out her name and shuddered against her, burying his face into the crook between her neck and her shoulder. And even broken into too many pieces to count, even thrown as she was off the side of a very high cliff and still floating her way down to earth, Dru understood that nothing was ever going to be the same again. Especially not her.

Cayo's version of enjoying himself in paradise, Dru was not greatly surprised to learn, involved cutting down his business hours to something like six or eight hours per day instead of more than twice that.

"What a great sacrifice this must be," she murmured toward the end of one such "holiday" afternoon as she took more dictation, her fingers flying across the keyboard when she would have preferred to explore him instead, not that he had asked. "To abandon yourself so hedonistically into a normal person's version of a workday."

Cayo eyed her, his dark eyes as hot as they were amused. In deference to the fact he'd decreed this a vacation—and, perhaps, all that had changed between them—he wore a white shirt he had not bothered to button, displaying his mouthwatering physique and olive complexion and making Dru glad she was so adept at touch-typing. She could stare at him without missing a single word. His feet were even propped up on the desk in front of him, completing the picture. He would have looked like indolence incarnate had he not been sitting in his office suite, composing lists of commands for his fleet of vice presidents the world over to obey as soon as Dru pressed Send.

"You are always welcome to distract me," he said after a moment.

She opened her mouth to offer a knee-jerk sort of demurral, but stopped herself. What was there to lose? Cayo's business would storm ahead the way it always did when these strange days were over, when she was gone. But she would never get another chance to have him like this. She had the sense again, as she had repeatedly since that first day here, that she was gathering up all these white-hot, deliriously passionate moments to hoard later, when she was alone. When she was free. When she had nothing but memories to hold on to.

"If you insist, Mr. Vila," she said now, watching that fierce light blaze in his eyes. She slid out of the chair she'd pulled up next to his desk and onto the floor, smiling slightly as his hard face tightened with desire.

Slowly, holding his gaze, she crawled between his legs.

"Is this a new form of taking dictation, Miss Bennett?" he asked, that dark amusement in his low voice, though she could hear the faint rasp in it that hinted at the fire within him, and she smiled, running her hands over his hard thighs, his taut abdomen. His legs thudded down on either side of her, caging her right where she wanted to be. "I'm a fan."

Then she reached into his soft trousers, lifting out the hard, smooth length of him and taking him deep in her mouth.

He groaned. And Dru worshipped him, tasting the velvet smoothness of him, loving him with her mouth, her tongue, her hands and her lips, bringing him to a roaring finish with his hands gripped tight in her hair.

It was these moments she was collecting, she told herself as he lifted her into his lap and kissed her hungrily, his heartbeat pounding hard beneath her as he held her against his chest. These moments when she could kid herself and pretend that he was hers.

They fell into a kind of pattern as the days passed. Cayo was still her boss, despite the dramatic change in their relationship, and Dru did not dispute that. What might have been untenable if she hadn't already planned to leave him was really more like a game when it was only her heart, not her career, at stake. So she was happy enough to continue performing her duties, with only cosmetic alterations.

"Don't do that thing with your hair," Cayo said one morning as she stepped out of the massive, glass-enclosed shower, complete with a window overlooking the ocean, that was its own room in the master suite's bath.

He stood in the door that led out into his bedroom, his dark eyes burning as they tracked over her, watching as she wrapped herself in a towel. He'd pulled on another pair of the linen trousers he favored in the warm weather, but no shirt, and all of that muscled masculine perfection on display made her feel overheated. Again.

They'd woken at dawn and gone for a swim in the quiet lagoon. He'd lifted her against him where he stood, simply pulled her bikini bottoms to the side and slid inside her, rocking them both to mindlessness in the clear, warm water, as the sun began to light the perfect sky above them.

She was still trembling slightly from the aftereffects.

"Don't do what with my hair?" she asked. It couldn't be healthy, wanting someone like this. She'd imagined sleeping with him would be a single act, a fix, the end of all that yearning and infatuation.

But instead, you made it worse, that voice inside was quick to remind her. As if she didn't know.

He made a vague gesture toward the back of his head. "That twist," he said. A strange expression crossed his face then, something she might have called vulnerability on another man—but that was impossible. This was Cayo. "I like it down around your shoulders," he said gruffly. "I like my hands in it."

And he'd turned and disappeared, leaving Dru to make of that what she would.

She pulled on the cheerful, bright blue-and-yellow maxidress she'd adopted as her uniform here, and ran her fingers through her hair as it settled around her shoulders in damp waves. She stared at herself in the large mirror that dominated the nearest wall, and hardly recognized herself. The exposure to the sun had brought out her freckles, and that sheen to her skin. Her eyes were bright, her mouth soft, somehow. And her dark hair tumbled all around her, still wet from her shower, giving her a sensual and sultry sort

of look. She was poles apart from the image of Dru
Bennett she'd prided herself on embodying in her five
years at the Vila Group: impeccably, quietly fashion-
able. Professional above all else.

She could lie and tell herself that it was the islands
doing this to her, turning her into a different person,
but she knew better. It was Cayo.

She just had to remember that it was temporary.

Back in London, Dru would never dress this way.
Just as she would never interrupt a dictation session as
she had the other day, or wear her hair down because a
man demanded it. Just as she would never sleep with
her boss, no matter how much she might have wanted
him, and then carry on working for him. But this was
Bora Bora, and it was as if what she did here didn't
count.

It's only a handful of days, she reminded herself now
as she walked to meet him in the office. *It will be like
none of this happened when I get back home.*

She told herself that the twisting feeling in her stomach was joy. That it was happiness that she was letting
herself do this, experience this, live in the moment
here, when it was so unlike her. She had her whole
life in front of her to regret this, after all. There was
no sense starting now.

But it was as if Cayo knew that there was something
she wasn't telling him—or perhaps he felt the pressure
of the temporary nature of this as well. Sometimes he
merely picked her up and held her against the nearest wall when he wanted her, his expression so fierce
as he thrust within her, as if he saw the same painful
future before him. Or he woke her again and again in
the night, to taste her, to touch her, to send her flying

over the edge. As if to prove he could. As if to make sure it was real.

One afternoon, after he'd ended their workday, he found her on the lanai outside the library. He stood in the entryway for a long moment, watching her, until Dru set her crime novel aside and gave him her full attention.

"Did you need something?" she asked, and smiled at him, ready for another series of commands. Plans for the next day's business, perhaps.

"I don't know how you do it." His voice was dark and low. It made a shiver of unease snake along the back of her neck.

"Read?" she asked mildly.

He ignored that.

"Your words, your smiles." He ran a hand along the jaw he shaved irregularly here, and looked not unlike a pirate as he gazed down at her, rakish and unapologetically lethal. But she didn't recognize that look in his eyes. "Even in my bed. There are a thousand places for you to hide, aren't there? And you do."

Her heart thudded hard against her ribs. And there was a kind of ringing in her ears, as if alarms were going off all around them. But she knew that wasn't true—there was only the sound of the waves as they crashed against the sand. The birds singing in the trees. The wind dancing through the chimes out on the terrace.

"I don't know what you mean."

"Do you know, I almost believe you."

He didn't look angry, or upset in any way. She could have handled either of those without blinking. He looked almost…resigned. All of that clever attention of his focused on her, and growing darker by the moment. And it was making her feel panicky. Desperate. Afraid, again, of what he might see.

"I'm not hiding." She stood, then opened up her arms, proving it. "I'm right here."

He smiled, and it had the usual effect of rendering her breathless, for all it was shaded as much with regret as with desire. She didn't want to know why.

"Are you, Dru?" he asked. But he closed the distance between them as if he found her as difficult to resist as she did him, and pulled her against him. "Are you really?"

Dru didn't answer. She kissed him instead. Hot. Desperate. With everything she was capable of giving him.

He didn't speak again.

He had her kneel on the small sofa, then took her from behind, his hands on her hips and his hard chest at her back as he thrust into her, making her sob out his name with only the glittering sea before them as witness.

And when he bent his head to her neck, spent in the aftermath of their passion, she murmured soothing words and told herself it was another victory. Another memory; hers to hoard.

CHAPTER EIGHT

THEY sat out on one of the patios one evening, surrounded by softly flickering candles, with the canopy of stars bright and astonishing above them. Dru leaned back in her chair and stared up at them, aware on some level that time was passing even in moments like this one, when she felt outside of time altogether.

Don't forget what temporary means, she advised herself. *Don't pretend that any of this can last.*

Across from her, Cayo was finishing a call with a CFO at one of his New York companies. He frowned out toward the dark ocean as he talked, his voice growing increasingly more impatient. Dru sipped at her wine and watched him, imprinting that impossible face into her memory, making sure she had memories enough to spare. That blade of a nose, that granite jaw. Her boss become her lover. Now that it had happened, it felt inevitable. As if they had always been headed here. As if the three years in between Cadiz and now had been part of some grander plan.

Just as she had always intended to leave him, eventually. Lest she forget her own plans. Her promises.

Victory, she chanted quietly in her own head. *This is a victory. I'll go home the winner at the end, and do exactly as I planned to do two weeks ago.*

But she wasn't sure she believed her own cheering squad.

The staff brought out plates of tuna tartare to start, and Dru took a bite, sighing with pleasure at the burst of flavor, the excruciatingly fresh taste. She took a sip of her wine. She smiled when Cayo ended his call and ignored the way he looked at her, so dark and brooding.

"It's fantastic," she told him. "You should have some."

"Are you working tonight, Dru?" His tone was cold, brusque. It lanced into her, as no doubt he intended it to do. "I thought we agreed that business ended at half five today. When I want you to perform in your role as perfect assistant, capable of any measure of small talk under any and all circumstances, I will let you know."

"Or don't have any," she said blandly. "More for me."

His mouth moved into a hard kind of curve, too intense to be a smile.

More courses appeared before them. Parrotfish stuffed with crab. Mahi-mahi in a sweet coconut curry. A platter of grilled shrimp and scallops, and another of artfully arranged sushi. The table was bright with all the colors, and the food looked almost too pretty to eat. Almost.

"Tell me something about you," he said when their plates were full, and there had been no sound for some time save the clink of silver against china and the ever-present crash of the ocean against the shore. "Something I don't know." He shook his head impatiently when she opened her mouth. "I don't mean anything on your CV, which you trot out by rote and which I know is stellar or I wouldn't have hired you."

Dru put down her fork and regarded him calmly for

a moment, while that same alarm inside her shrieked anew. There was no reason he should want to "know something" about her. She needed to change the subject, redirect his attention. He had enough weapons to use against her as it was. Why add to his arsenal?

"What is it you want to know?" she asked, warily. She picked up her wine, pressed the glass to her lips and then decided she already felt too unbalanced. There was no need to throw alcohol in the mix and make it that much worse. "Is this when we discuss our lists of past lovers? Mine is shorter than yours. Obviously."

His dark amber eyes gleamed, as if he appreciated her attempt to focus the conversation back on him, and what was, she was all too aware, an impressive and lengthy list indeed. But he didn't take the bait. He only smiled slightly, and speared a plump shrimp on the sharp tines of his fork.

"You personally witnessed the ignoble end of my family, such as it was," he said, his voice as low as his gaze was intent, and something about it shivered through her, making her ache for him in a different way. "What of yours? You never speak of them. I assume you did not spring full-grown from an office-supply warehouse, brandishing one of those gray suits of yours like a weapon."

The expression on his face said he wasn't entirely sure about that. Dru cleared her throat and recognized that she was stalling. She couldn't seem to help it. There had been a time when she would have been thrilled to encourage his interest in her—any interest at all. But not now. Not when she had a much greater sense of how hard it was going to be to leave him already. What would it be like if he really knew all of her? How would she survive losing him then?

"Did you encourage personal chatter about the office all these years and I missed it?" she asked lightly. He inclined his head, awarding her the point, but he still waited expectantly. He was still not distracted from his question. *Damn him.* She set her wine back on the glass-topped table, feeling jerky and uneven. Unduly defensive. "We lived in Shropshire, in a village outside Shrewsbury, until my father died. Dominic and I were barely five years old." She saw his brows knit together and nodded. "Twins, yes. We moved around a good bit after that. In the end, it was a relief to go to university and stay in one place for a few years."

"Why did you move around so much?" he asked. If she didn't know better, she would think he was fascinated. That he really wanted to know the answer. And maybe that was why she told him—because, despite everything, she wanted to believe that he could want that, and that trumped even her heightened sense of self-preservation. To say nothing of her sense, full stop.

"My mum had a lot of boyfriends," she said, which was more than she usually told anyone. It was amazing how easy it was to strip all those hard, dark years of the fear and the tears and simply cram it all into one little sentence that barely hinted at either. "Some became stepfathers."

She had no intention of telling him anything further. But when she dared meet his gaze again, he was looking back at her the way he always did. Dark eyes in that warrior's face, brooding and *intent.* As if she was a mystery he wanted to puzzle out. And would.

"My mother also remarried, I suppose you could say," he said then, in that dry way of his that hinted at a dark humor she'd never imagined he could possess. Or had thought she'd only imagined lurked in him on that one night in Cadiz. She would miss it. She could tell. "But as she is now a bride of Christ we are not meant to complain."

Dru couldn't help but smile, and his eyes warmed in return, and she knew then that she was going to tell him things she'd never breathed to another soul. Because she still wanted him to know her, despite how temporary this was. Despite the very real fear that it would give him too much power over her. She wanted to imagine, when he was on to his next assistant, ensconced on one of his yachts with his next blonde supermodel, that he would remember her, too. And when he did—*if* he did—she wanted this to have mattered. And that meant sharing parts of herself she'd never let anyone else see.

"They were always violent." She was surprised how little her voice shook, and how easy it was to look at him and forget what she'd been through. How safe he made her feel, simply by not looking away. As if that simple act shared the burden of it, somehow. "To Mum, and then increasingly to Dominic. I was quite good at not being seen."

"I believe you," he said, an undercurrent in his voice. "You still are."

"But then I got older," she said. She was far too captivated by the way he watched her, as if he was supporting her that simply, that completely, to respond to the strange thing he said. She filed it away. "And they started to notice me more." She swallowed, then shook her head slightly, as if to shake away the memories. His gaze darkened. Hardened. "There was one named Harold who was the worst. Always trying to get me alone. Always quick to stick his hands where he shouldn't. But when I told Mum she slapped my face and called me a liar and a whore." Dru shrugged, almost as if that memory didn't still sting. Almost as if she was so tough it hardly registered, when the truth was, she'd never said that out loud before. Not like that. "So when I could, I left. The last time I saw her I was nineteen."

The only other person she'd shared her dark history with was Dominic, and they'd always used their own shorthand—never quite mentioning the facts of what had happened so much as the effects. She'd never told any of her mates at university, or even the small handful of boyfriends she'd had back when she'd still had time for a social life. It had seemed so private, and so terribly shameful, and her mates had all been about having a laugh, not dredging up the horrors of Dru's childhood. She'd enjoyed them precisely *because* they weren't the sort for intimate confidences or bared souls. It meant hers were safe.

She jerked her gaze away from Cayo's now, reaching blindly for her wine, no longer caring what it might do to her. It was better than what *he* was doing to her simply by listening. By making her feel safe when there was no such thing. She knew that better than most.

"And your brother?" Cayo asked after a moment. "Your twin? You're not close with him either?"

It shocked her. It felt like a kick in the stomach, an attack, and her first reaction was pure, unadulterated fury. And then, if she was honest, a lot of it was that same old, terrible guilt she always felt where Dominic was concerned.

"Not as such, thanks," she snapped at Cayo, not caring if she was being unfair. "As he's dead."

And then she hated herself. So deeply and so comprehensively it made her feel ill. She slid the wineglass back onto the table and wrapped her arms around her middle, certain she needed help to keep herself together.

Cayo didn't look away. He gave no indication that he minded that she'd snapped at him like that, out of nowhere. He simply sat much too still and much too close across the table, watching her fall apart.

"I'm sorry," he began after a moment, his voice calm.

"No," she interrupted him, her words feeling thick in her mouth. "I'm sorry. I shouldn't have said it like that. How would you know? Only it was rather recent and I've still not managed to figure out how to talk about it. About him."

"Recent?" Cayo frowned then. He looked as close to confused as she'd ever seen him. "What do you mean by recent? I don't recall you taking any time off."

In the past five years. He didn't have to say that part. It was understood.

"Time off?" She shook her head, then let out a hollow little sound, not really a laugh at all. "It's not as if you give out any personal time, Cayo. I can't imagine even having asked for time off. Look how you reacted to my resignation."

That muscle leapt in his jaw, betraying his temper. His eyes went black with something that looked again like pain. Tortured and grim, the way he'd looked that night in Milan. It made her want to reach over and touch him, soothe him. And once more, she deeply regretted her words the moment they hung in the sweet night air between them, but she couldn't seem to stop herself. And she couldn't take them back.

"Yes," he said after a moment in a deep, rough voice she hardly recognized. "Of course. I am such a heartless monster that I would keep you from your brother's funeral, purely out of spite."

Her own heart seemed to tighten at that, and she shook her head. "That's not what I meant."

"After all," he continued in the same dark and bitter tone that made her want to weep and to protect him, somehow, from whatever made him sound that way, even if it was her, "what do I know of family? You are the only person in the world who knows how little regard my own grandfather held for me. You heard him. You are also the only person in the world who has maintained any kind of close relationship with me for any length of time." His smile then hurt to see. "You would certainly know how little qualified I am to speak on the subject of families."

She felt awful, and it moved in her like heat. Like fear. And she couldn't stand it.

"Don't be an idiot," she said, almost crossly.

He froze. His dark eyes widened.

"I said I doubted you would give me time off," she said, very distinctly. "You are a demanding boss, Cayo. You insist on round-the-clock availability and access. I had no reason to think you would greet the news that I even *had* a personal life with anything but horror."

"You have no idea what I would do," he replied tightly.

"I know exactly what you would do," she retorted. "It's what you pay me for. What you offered me three times my salary and the private island of my choice for, if memory serves."

For a moment he only looked at her. The moment stretched out between them, and despite what she'd just told him, Dru had no idea how he would react. None at all.

And then, impossibly, proving how little she knew him after all, he threw back his head and laughed.

She'd never known he *could* laugh. It was an infectious sound. Joy moved across his hard, fierce face, the laughter lighting him up, changing him, changing *her*—

The truth slammed into her, stealing her breath, making her head spin. The scales fell from her eyes, and hard—so hard they seemed to bruise her on their way down.

She was in love with him.

And quite clearly, she had been for a very long time.

Once again, she'd been fooling herself. She'd called it an "infatuation," called it her "feelings for him." She'd minimized it in her own head, worrying only that this trip would take recovering from. She hadn't dared so much as think the truth. Meanwhile, she'd chosen to lose herself in his life. She'd never thought to ask why she'd been passed over for that other job three years ago even though she'd known perfectly well she'd been qualified for it. Worse, she'd chosen to keep her distance from her brother—when he'd died, but even before, if she was honest. It was easier to send money from afar than it was to roll around in the messes Dominic had made, though it hurt her to admit she'd done exactly that. She'd done all of it.

All to cater to and care for a man who would never love her back. Who hadn't the slightest idea what love *was.*

Then again, came that voice inside her, brutal and unflinching, *do you?*

The world seemed to tilt around her wildly, sickeningly, as if she'd found herself trapped on some carnival fun ride. She felt a terrible shame wash through her, scalding her. She'd wanted her damaged, selfish mother to love her as she should have done. She'd wanted all of those stepfathers to love her like a daughter. She'd wanted Dominic to love her more than his addictions. And Cayo… He couldn't love anything, could he? So she'd settled for making him *need* her instead. And she'd thought he valued her for that, if nothing else.

Was that what she'd wanted, in his office that day that seemed so long ago now? Had some part of her believed she would fling her resignation at him, still smarting from the printed email she'd found, and he would leap to his feet and declare his love for her?

Of course he hadn't. No one ever had, and Cayo wouldn't know how, even if he did feel the things she did. Her entire life was a great and complicated monument to deeply pathetic, sadly epic, and wholly unrequited love.

She was such a fool.

And he was watching her now, that unexpected laughter still on his face, making him more than simply beautiful in that hard, fierce way—making him handsome, too. Almost approachable.

It broke what was left of her heart.

"Are you all right?" he asked, his eyes still bright as they searched hers, sharpening as they saw whatever must have been there—the truth, she feared. The terrible truth she could never, ever let him know.

She didn't know how she did it.

"I'm fine," she managed to say. He frowned, no doubt at that shaky note in her voice that made her sound anything at all but *fine,* so she gestured at her mouth, and lied. "I've bit my tongue, that's all."

* * *

Time, it turned out, was the one thing Cayo couldn't control.

It was the afternoon of her final day—which neither one of them had mentioned directly yet, though it hung there between them no matter how many times he'd taken her the night before, or this morning—and he could not bring himself to pay attention the conference call that she was participating in as his representative. He sat next to her at the small table in the office, his legs stretched out before him, and found he could do nothing at all but watch her as she spoke into the speaker phone in the center of the table.

"I'll be certain to bring that to Mr. Vila's attention," she said, in that smooth and capable voice of hers that, now he knew what lay behind it, made him burn. "But in the meantime, I think we need to take another look at those figures before we jump to any conclusions."

Maybe it was that he could see her, when the rest of the people on the call could not. No doubt they pictured the usual Dru, in her sleek suits and dangerous heels, her hair tamed and twisted out of view. But he saw the real Dru. Wild hair and that hint of color on her pale skin, the dusting of freckles across her nose and shoulders. Bare feet and a turquoise sarong wrapped around a hot pink bikini. Not in the least bit professional, not that anyone could have told that from her cool voice.

She was magnificent. She was his. And she was going to leave him.

He didn't know what he was going to do about that, he only knew he couldn't allow it. He wouldn't.

But he also knew he'd run out of options.

She propped her head up with one hand as she listened to the call, the various executives talking over each other, all of them completely unaware that Cayo was listening to them dither and bicker. He'd found that it could be highly educational to use Dru in this way, to make them think they were talking to someone far more approachable than Cayo ever was. He'd found it helped ferret out all manner of truths.

He wished the same could be said of Dru herself.

"Mr. Vila prefers to be offered potential solutions when presented with problems, Barney," she said into the speaker. "I can certainly raise your concerns to him, but I suspect he's going to give you a similar reply. Only he won't be quite as polite."

There was some laughter, and she glanced over to smile at him, her gray eyes sparkling nearly silver. *Real,* he thought with satisfaction. Not one of her work smiles she trotted out to placate or soothe him from time to time, all of which he'd come to hate. But even so, he knew she was still hiding from him. He didn't know what, or why, but he could see the secrets in her eyes. Even now.

Perversely, it only made him want her more.

He'd told her that she was the only person he'd ever had any kind of close relationship with, and the stark truth of that haunted him. She was the only person alive that he had ever trusted. He had allowed her unparalleled access to all parts of his life. To him. No employee had ever been so entrenched in his personal life before and he had certainly never allowed one of his women anywhere near his business. Only Dru bridged those worlds. Only Dru.

And his time with her was almost up.

Giving in to an urge he hardly understood, as if it might ease the sudden heaviness in his chest, Cayo reached over and took her hand. Her eyes flew to his, but he concentrated on the slide of her fingers against

his. The way they fitted together so well, even here.
He brought her hand up to his lips and pressed a kiss to
the back of it. She curved her palm to better fit against
his mouth, his jaw, as if she was holding him too, and
something shifted inside him. A wall he hadn't known
was there tumbled down, and he knew, then, what he
must do.

There was one way to keep her. One strategy he
hadn't tried. It would keep her close. With him. And
so what if it wouldn't be precisely as it had been? It
was good enough. He might even like having her as
his family, whatever that word really meant. She was
the closest thing to it he'd ever known.

He just had to get her to say yes.

"The helicopter will be here in two hours," Dru said
the following morning, careful to sound calm. Matter-
of-fact. "The plane will be ready to go once we get to
Tahiti."

Cayo stood at the end of the pier, with his back to
her. He looked remote, forbidding and still, she wanted
to lean into all of that broad strength, rest her head
against his shoulder blade. She wanted to let the pure,
male scent of him surround her. She wanted to soak
in his heat like the sun. Her bare toes curled into the
smooth, warm wood beneath her feet and she told herself she was fine. That she felt nothing but relief that it
was all almost over, with only the long plane ride left
to survive. *Perfectly fine.*

They had woken up at dawn, wrapped around each
other in Cayo's huge bed. He had pulled her over
him before she was wholly awake, sliding into her
so smoothly she'd wondered whether it was real or a
dream. *Or goodbye,* a harsher voice in her head had

suggested. She'd ignored it, leaned down to him and kissed him.

Slowly, they'd explored each other. Long, drugging kisses and endless touches, building a different kind of flame. One that burned long and sweet. One that danced and seduced and drew out the perfection of each caress. One that made them both sigh out their pleasure when it turned white-hot and wild all around them.

Dru felt the glowing embers of that same fire inside her, even now. She'd almost been afraid to track Cayo down after she'd confirmed their arrangements—as if she thought he could see straight through her to that place that would never stop burning for him. That place he could ignite with so little effort—a look, a touch. Would that ever fade? Would time without him dim it? Somehow, she doubted it.

"I suppose no one can stay in paradise forever, can they?" she asked brightly when he didn't turn to face her, trying to make conversation—anything to cover her own nervousness. Anything to pretend it didn't hurt.

"Don't." It was hard. Fierce.

"It's so lovely here." She felt helpless. Unable to stop. "But it's not real, is it?"

He turned then, so dark and ruthless, dressed in no more than a pair of white loose trousers and still, so dangerous. She almost took a step back to keep him from looming over her, but she restrained herself. His eyes slammed into hers.

"But this is?" His accent was more pronounced than usual, and she felt it inside, like an echo. "Your deliberately inane chatter? Surely you know by now that it won't work on me."

That might have stung—it did—but Dru couldn't let herself fall into that trap. There would be no fighting that led to kissing, no explosions of temper or passion or anything else. No shoes. No jumping from the pier. She wouldn't let him sabotage her departure. More importantly, she wouldn't let herself do the same.

"You are far too busy to spend any more time hiding away from the world," she said, and that wasn't idle conversation or flattery. It was the simple truth. He was who he was. "Even here."

"As you pointed out to me only last night," he said gruffly, "the point of hiring the best people in the world is occasionally to delegate responsibilities to them."

"I did say that." She smiled, but it felt hollow. He didn't return it. And last night felt so far away now. As if it belonged to other people. "Cayo…"

She bit her lip and watched his dark amber eyes turn nearly black with a mixture of pain and passion, and her heart seemed to squeeze tight in her chest. If she started crying now, she worried she would never stop. She tried to shove that dangerous ache away.

"Don't make this harder than it has to be," she whispered.

Still, he only stared back at her, as if he were hewn from stone. He looked powerful beyond measure, ruthless and fierce and she thought it might kill her to leave him. That thing inside her that had no pride, no respect, no boundaries whatsoever, might physically take her down as she tried to walk away. Her little masochist within, who wanted him and only him, however she could have him. Whatever that meant.

However much it hurt.

"It doesn't have to be hard," he said then.

His voice was low, and there was an intense light

deep in the dark of his gaze. He reached over and traced a lazy pattern just above the waistband of her linen trousers, where there was a gap between them and her top. She sucked in a breath, so attuned to him that even that faintest touch unleashed the fire in her, made her body ready itself for him, as if on command. When he looked at her again, there was gold in his eyes and the faintest curve on that cruel mouth of his.

"I think you should marry me," he said.

The world stopped.

No breath. No sound. No air.

But somehow, she didn't faint. She didn't fall. She only stood there, staring back at him. "What did you just say?"

"Don't play that game." He took her chin in his hand, his gaze piercing into her, seeing far too much—and she couldn't allow that. She wouldn't survive it if he knew she loved him. Dru jerked her head back, and he let go, but not without reminding them both, wordlessly, that he'd allowed it.

"You can't be serious," she said, her breath, her voice—all of her ragged. Uneven. Trembling as if what he'd said was some kind of earthquake and she was still swaying in the aftermath.

"I have never been more serious in my life," he grated out, his dark eyes flashing.

And this, she found, hurt worst of all. It was everything she'd ever wanted—more than she'd dreamed possible—but not like this. Never like this. Two weeks ago he'd tricked her onto that plane, claiming they were bound for Zurich. This was no different.

It just hurt more.

"No," she said, her voice barely a whisper. "I can't."

"Why not?" It was the voice he used to do business, to make deals. To convince whoever dared say no to him that they should change their answer—and they usually did.

Dru felt bruised. Battered. Torn apart by what she knew was the right thing to do, and that treacherous part of her that wanted him however she could get him. Why couldn't she simply jump at this chance, her masochistic side wondered. He might learn to love her. Maybe he already did, in as much as he was able. And wasn't *maybe* good enough?

But there was another voice in there now, a new one. Fragile and tiny, but hers.

"I deserve better," she heard herself say.

The effect on Cayo was immediate and dramatic, though he didn't seem to move. It was as if all that power, all that ferocity, was suddenly burning in his exotic eyes while the rest of him went terribly, alarmingly still. As if she'd wounded him beyond measure.

"'Better'?" he echoed.

Dru's hands shot out, as if to touch him, to hold him, but at the final moment she found she didn't dare. Her throat was thick with grief, her chest hurt, and there was nothing she could do. She couldn't make this better—and he was making it worse.

"I have a promise to keep to my brother," she whispered. "Nothing is more important than that."

Not even you, she thought miserably, while everything inside her revolted.

"Marry me." But it was less a command than a plea, wrapped up though it was in his ruthless delivery. "It's the only solution." When she only stared back at him through eyes that grew blurrier by the moment, he looked almost desperate. "I don't know how to lose you," he said, his voice near a whisper. "I can't."

"You'll have to learn," she managed to push out past the constriction in her throat.

"Dru—"

"I can't settle, Cayo." She threw that out, through the riot inside of her, through the tears that threatened. And it just kept hurting more. "Not even for you."

"Dru."

Even the way he said her name hurt. As if she was the one who'd mortally wounded him. He reached over and took her face in his hands, and that was when she noticed the tears wetting her cheeks, despite her best efforts.

But he didn't love her. He didn't even pretend. Not even now, to marry her. To keep her. *He didn't love her.* So she could tear herself into pieces by leaving now, or she could stay with him and marry him and fall apart by degrees, year by loveless year, until she really did hate him the way she'd only wished she could two weeks ago.

"I am not the monster you think I am," he said, soft and dark and straight into her heart, like a knife.

"Your two weeks are up, Cayo." It was the hardest thing she'd ever done. The greatest sacrifice she'd ever made. She stepped back, watched his hands drop away, and knew she would never be whole again. "You have to let me go."

CHAPTER NINE

IF this was what it was like to *care,* Cayo thought some weeks after he'd returned from Bora Bora and Dru had left him on the tarmac without a backward glance, he had been right to discourage the practice for the whole of his adult life.

When I decide to sabotage you, she had told him once, *there will be nothing the least bit passive about it.* He couldn't help but wonder if this was what she'd meant. This…aching sense of loss that colored everything a dull gray.

He hated it.

He glared at one of his many vice presidents across the wide expanse of his London desk, and managed, somehow, to refrain from wringing the man's neck.

"I don't understand why I'm having this conversation," he said coldly. The other man winced. Cayo drummed his fingers on the glossy expanse of his desktop. "Surely I hired you to make decisions at this level yourself."

He was being far kinder than he felt. Personable, even. But he knew he was measuring himself against the kind of results Dru could have wrung out of this man with a few smiles and a supportive word or two and, by that tally, he was a failure.

That was something he was getting used to, however gracelessly. And she still wasn't here. She had disappeared completely after his plane had touched down on British soil, just as she'd promised she would. He supposed he hadn't believed it would happen, that she would really do it. He still didn't.

"Of course, of course, I would be happy—" the vice president in front of him stammered out. "It's only that you always wanted to hear every detail of every potential negotiation before—"

"That was before," Cayo said, and sighed. He rubbed at his temples and tried to stop glaring. "If there's nothing else…?"

He sat back in his mighty chair behind his massive desk and watched the other man sprint for the safety of the outer office. And then, like clockwork, his new assistant appeared in the doorway to update him on his schedule and his messages.

Claire was everything anyone could want in a personal assistant, he thought then, eyeing her. The agency had placed her the day he'd arrived back from French Polynesia, and she'd acquitted herself beautifully in the weeks since. She was a quick learner. She was eager to please and yet didn't tremble every time he spoke, like so many of his executives. She was even pleasant enough to look at, in a very blond and vaguely Nordic sort of way, which he knew always put the potential investors and various clients at ease. She'd been with him a month now and he had yet to detect a single flaw.

Save one. She wasn't Dru. She hardly knew how he took his coffee, much less how to finesse his fractious and demanding board of directors with seeming ease and nonchalance. He didn't ask for her thoughts on delicate business negotiations. He would never trust her to have his interests at heart while tending to long calls filled with unhappy executives. Claire was, he supposed, a perfectly decent personal assistant.

Which forced him to consider the fact that Dru had been far more than that. She'd been more like a partner. And she was gone now, as if she'd never been at Vila Group at all. As if she'd never been with him.

What had he expected? He kept asking himself the same question, and there was never any answer. *Dru hated him.* She'd told him so. Had he really believed that sex could change that? Or that it might change who he was—who he had always been? This monster who did not even know when he was crushing the life out of the only thing he'd ever really cared about?

"Mr. Vila?" Claire asked. A note in her voice suggested it was not the first time she'd said his name. "Shall I get Mr. Young on the phone for you?"

He was not himself. He had not been for some weeks now, and well did he know it.

"Yes," Cayo muttered. It wasn't her fault she wasn't Dru. He had to keep reminding himself of this. Several times a day. "Fine."

He dealt with the call with his usual lack of tact or mercy and when it was done, found himself at the great wall of windows that looked out over the City. He had been scowling out at the depressingly typical British rain for several minutes before it occurred to him that he'd been doing too much of this lately. Brooding like a moody adolescent.

He was disgusted with himself. Had he moped when his grandfather had tossed him out? He had not. After an initial moment to absorb what had happened, he had walked off that mountain and built a life for himself. He hadn't mourned. He hadn't *brooded*. He'd focused and he'd worked hard, and in time, he'd come to think of his grandfather's betrayal as the best thing that had happened to him. Where would he be without it?

But, of course, he knew. He would have been a cobbler like his grandfather in that pretty little white-washed town, living out a simple life beneath the red roofs, smiling at the tourists who snapped pictures and paid too much for their restaurant meals. Suffering through the whispers and the gossip that would never have subsided, no matter how diligently he worked to combat them, no matter what he did. Paying and paying for his mother's sins, forever and ever without end. He let out a derisive snort at the thought.

I am better off, he told himself. Then told himself he believed it. *Then and now.*

But even so, he stared out the window and saw Dru instead.

They'd sprawled on a blanket on the sandy beach together one night in Bora Bora, wearing nothing but the bright, full moon beaming down from above them. Dru had been nestled against his shoulder, her breath still uneven from the heady passion they'd indulged in, scattering their clothes across the beach in their haste. Their insatiable need.

"I'll admit it," Cayo had said. "I never had a pet quite like you before."

"No?" He'd heard laughter in her voice, though he could only see the top of her head. "Do I sit and stay better than all the rest?"

"I was thinking how much I enjoy it when you surrender," he'd murmured. Hadn't he had her sobbing out his name only a few moments before? He'd been teasing her—something he'd only just realized was reserved for her alone, but when she'd shifted position so she could look at him, her gaze had been serious.

"Careful what you wish for," she'd said softly, in a voice that didn't match the look in her eyes.

"I don't know what you mean," he'd said, reaching out to curl a dark wave of her hair behind her ear, reveling in the thick silk of it between his fingers. "There is nothing wrong with surrender. Particularly to me."

"Easy for you to say." Her voice had been wry. "You've never had the pleasure."

He'd smiled, but then the moment had seemed darker, somehow. Or more honest, perhaps.

"Is that what you're afraid of?" he'd asked quietly.

She'd let out a small sound, as if she'd almost laughed, and then looked away.

"My brother was an addict," she'd said, her voice small, but determined. "I don't know why it feels like I'm betraying him to tell you that. It's true."

Cayo had said nothing. He'd only stroked her back, held her close, and listened. She'd told him about Dominic's attempts at recovery, about his inevitable falls from grace. She'd told him about the way it had been before, when she'd worked in other jobs, and had dropped them to rush to Dominic's side, only to find herself heartbroken and lied to, again and again. And occasionally sacked, to boot. She'd told him about the good times peppered in with the bad. About how close she'd been to her twin once, how for a long time the only thing they'd had in the world had been each other.

"But that wasn't quite true, because he also had his addictions," she'd said. "And he always surrendered to them, eventually. No matter how much he claimed he didn't want to. And then one day he just couldn't come back."

He'd turned then, rolling her over to her back so he could gaze down at her, searching her face, her eyes. But she'd been as unreadable as ever. Still hiding in plain sight, her gray eyes shadowed tonight, and darker than they should have been.

She'd reached out, then, carefully, as if he was something precious to her. She'd traced the line of his jaw, his nose, even the shape of his brows with her fingertips, then run them over his lips, her mouth curving slightly when he'd nipped at her.

"I wonder what that's like?" she'd whispered then, and he'd seen something like agony in her eyes, there and then gone. "Unable to resist the very thing you know will destroy you. Drawn to it, despite yourself."

"Dru," he'd said, frowning down at her. "Surely you can't think—"

But she hadn't let him finish. She'd silenced him with a searingly hot kiss and then moved against him, seducing him that easily. He'd forgotten all about it, until now.

Had she been warning him? Had she known that she would get into his blood like this, poisoning him from the inside out, making him a stranger to himself? Cayo frowned out the window now, through the rain lashing across the glass. For the first time in almost twenty years, he wondered if it was worth it, this great empire he'd built and on which he focused to the exclusion of all else. Lately he wondered if, given the chance, he would trade it in. If he would take her instead.

Not that she'd offered him any such choice.

His intercom buzzed loudly behind him. He didn't move. He didn't know, any more, if he was furious or if he was simply the wreckage of the man he'd been. And he didn't like it, either way.

It took everything he had not to sic his team of investigators on her, not to have her every move reported back to him, wherever she was now, like the jealous, obsessive fool she'd once accused him of being. He'd been fighting the same near-overwhelming urge for weeks. She'd told him he needed to learn how to lose her, and he'd found it was not a lesson he was at all interested in mastering. The truth was, Cayo had never been any good at losing.

You have to let me go, she'd said. And he had, though it had nearly killed him, kept him up at nights and ruined his days. She was the one thing he'd ever given up on. The one thing he'd let slip through his hands.

And that felt like the greatest failure of all.

Cayo couldn't forgive himself. For any of it. Or her, for doing this to him. For turning him into this weak, destroyed creature, not at all who he'd believed himself to be, before.

Worst of all, for making him *care.*

Dru hadn't had time to collapse into the fetal position under her duvet once she'd made it back to her tiny bedsit in Clapham from the rainy tarmac where she'd last seen Cayo, despite the fact that was all she wanted to do.

Her already-booked flight straight back to Bora Bora had been leaving in two days' time. She'd met with Cayo's studiously blank-faced attorneys on the morning before her flight, and she'd signed whatever they'd put in front of her, not caring if it took blood and her firstborn, so long as it ensured her freedom. Finally. It had been the last necessary step.

And more than that, it had meant he was letting her go.

Some part of her had imagined he might pull his Godzilla routine. Roar and smash, grab and hoard. Demand another two weeks. Trap her into that marriage he'd proposed. *Something.* But he'd let her walk away from him at the airport. There had been nothing but a look in his eyes that she'd never seen before, turning all of that dark amber nearly black and eating her alive inside. The cold, dull, gray English day around them had been so depressingly *real life* she'd almost wondered if Bora Bora, the yacht in the Adriatic, Milan, and everything that had happened between them had been no more than a fevered dream.

The attorneys had been real, however, sliding papers at her one after the next in the Costa Coffee near Clapham Junction. She'd signed the last five years of her life away with every pen stroke. At his command. With his blessing.

Cayo Vila, who never gave in, who had never heard the word *no,* had let her go, at last.

Just as she'd told him to do, she'd reminded herself. Just as she'd asked.

And then she'd gone back home, carefully taken the tin that held Dominic's ashes, taped it shut and wrapped it up, and packed it away in her checked bag.

The trip had been brutal. When she'd finally staggered into her hotel on the southern part of Bora Bora's main island, far away from Cayo's private island, it had been impossible not to notice the differences. She'd told herself she didn't care. That she'd come for a specific reason and to perform a specific task, and when had she become such a princess that she found her rather smallish room that faced a bit of garden *depressing?* It was still a garden in Bora Bora.

She'd been furious with herself—and with Cayo—

for spoiling her so thoroughly. She'd become used to all of the luxury he surrounded himself with, apparently. It had only served to make her that much more appalled at herself and all the many ways she'd let herself down.

It had taken her a week to get up her nerve—and, if she was honest, to recover a little bit from those two intense weeks she'd spent with Cayo. But finally she'd been ready. One evening, at sunset, she'd taken one of the kayaks out and brought Dominic's ashes with her. As the sky exploded in oranges and pinks, she'd tipped his ashes out into the beautiful, peaceful lagoon.

And while she'd kept her promise to the first man she'd ever loved, and always would, she'd talked to him.

"I wish I could have saved you," she'd whispered to the water, the sky, the sea beyond. "I wish I'd tried harder."

She'd remembered her brother's delighted laughter that she'd never heard enough of. She'd thought of his wickedly amused gray eyes, so much brighter and more alive than hers—and then, sometimes, so much duller. She thought of his too-lean form, his shaggy dark hair, his poet's hands, and the tattoo on his shoulder of two hummingbirds that was, he'd once said with his cheeky grin, meant to represent the two of them. Free and in flight, forever.

"I wish I knew what happened to that picture of us as babies," she'd said, smiling at the memory of the old photograph. "I still don't know which one of us was which."

She'd mourned. She'd thought of their mother, so terrified of being on her own that any man had done, no matter how vicious. She'd thought of all those years when it had been Dominic and Dru against the world,

and how much she'd miss that for the rest of her life.
He'd taken something from her she could never get
back, and as she floated out there with jagged Mount
Otemanu before her and the world she knew so far
away, she'd let herself weep for the family she'd lost,
her potential children who would never know their
uncle, the whole rest of her life stretching out before
her with nothing of her twin in it except what she carried with her. In her.

Which wasn't enough, she'd thought then, bitterly.
It would never be enough.

"You took part of me with you, Dominic," she'd told
him as the inky darkness fell. "And I'll never forget
you. I promise."

And when all his ashes were gone she'd made her
way back to her hotel, where, finally, she'd curled up
on the bed, pulled the duvet over her head, and fallen
apart.

She'd stayed there for days. She'd cried until she'd
felt blinded by her own tears, until she'd made herself
retch from the force of her sobs. She'd let it all out, at
last, the terrible storm she'd been carrying with her
all this time. The grief of so many years, the pain and
the fury and all the lies she'd told herself about her
motivations. How much she'd loved Dominic and yes,
to her shame, how much she'd sometimes hated him,
too. His excuses and his promises, his grand plans that
never amounted to anything and his pretty, pretty lies
that she'd so desperately wanted to believe. She'd wept
for everything she'd lost, and how alone she was, and
how little she knew what to do with herself now that
she had nothing left to survive, no purpose to fulfill,
no great sacrifice remaining to build her life around.

But one day she sat up, and opened all the windows.

She let the breeze in, sweet with flowers and the sea.
She breathed in, deeply. She had her tea out on the hotel's pretty beach, and felt born again. Made new. As
if she really had put Dominic to rest.

Which meant it was time to face the truth about her
feelings for Cayo.

"Am I so scary?" he'd asked so long ago that night
in Cadiz. The restaurant had been noisy and crowded,
and his arm had brushed against hers as they sat so
close together at the tiny table. His unforgettable eyes
had still been so sad, but there was a curve to that cruel
mouth of his, and Dru had felt giddy, somehow. As if
they were both lit up with the magic of this night when
everything, she'd been sure, was changing.

"I think you take pride in being as scary as possible," she'd replied, smiling. "You have a reputation to
uphold, after all."

"I am certain that somewhere beneath it all, I am
nothing but clay, waiting to be molded by whoever happens along," he'd said, that near-smile deepening at the
absurdity of a man like him being swayed by anything
at all save his own inclination.

"Metal that might, under certain circumstances, be
welded, perhaps," she'd said, laughing. "Never clay."

"I bow to your superior knowledge," he'd said,
swirling his sherry in his glass, his gaze oddly intent
on hers. She'd felt herself flush with heat, and had felt
out of control. Reckless. Yet it had felt right, even so.
More right than she could remember anything else feeling, maybe ever. He'd leaned close, then murmured
close to her ear. "What would I do without you?"

She knew what he'd do without her, Dru thought
now, staring up at the perfect sky and the glorious lagoon, neither of which seemed to be as bright as they'd

been before. Without Cayo. He was probably doing
it right now—carrying on being Cayo Vila, scary by
design, taking whatever he wanted and expanding his
holdings on a whim.

But she was distorted by his absence. Disfigured.
And it didn't seem to get any better, no matter how
many days passed.

She sat in her cramped seat on an Air Vila flight
from Los Angeles to London, staring at the picture
of him on the back of the in-flight magazine, and she
thought her heart might tear itself apart in her chest.

I can't do this, she thought then, scraping away the
tears before they fell on her snoring seatmate. She
couldn't live out whatever life it was she thought she
ought to live, knowing that he was out there, knowing
that she would only ever see him in these painful, far-
away glimpses. On the telly, perhaps. In the magazines.
But never again right in front of her. Never again close
enough to touch, to taste, to tease.

She'd been in love with him for so long. She was
still in love with him, however hard she wished it away.
It hadn't changed. She was starting to believe it never
would. She felt minimized. Diminished, somehow,
without him. As if she'd depended on him just as much
as he'd depended on her all this time.

Back in her bedsit in London, she tried to tell herself that her whole life was ahead of her. That she need
only pick a path to follow and the world was hers. She
woke the morning after her return and scanned the papers, looking for clues to her next chapter—but it all
seemed cold and empty. Pointless.

She was haunted by Cayo even now, in a tiny flat
he'd never visited, on a bright morning that shouldn't
have had anything at all to do with him. Her eyes

drifted shut as she stood at her small refrigerator, and she saw him. Dark amber eyes. That fierce, ruthless face, with that blade of a nose and his cruel, impossible mouth. She *felt* him. She couldn't breathe without imagining his hands on her skin, his smile, the sound of his voice as he said her name. And that same old fire still burned within her, stubborn and hot, even now.

Did it really matter how he wanted her, as long as he did? Dru found herself pacing the small space that was her kitchen in agitation. She wished he'd handled it differently back in Bora Bora. She wished he'd lied and told her he wanted her, needed her—and not only as his assistant. She might not have believed him, but she'd have wanted to. And maybe it would have been enough.

But she couldn't marry him when he couldn't even pretend to love her. It turned out that was her line in the sand. Her single remaining boundary.

"A girl has to have some standards," she said out loud, shaking her head at herself. At the things she'd clung to all her life, like her belief that she would never be like her mother—and here she was, alone in her flat, halfway to Miss Havisham, arguing her way back to a man who could never love her the way she deserved to be loved.

But that was the problem. Dru didn't simply want to be loved. She wanted to be loved *by Cayo.* And she couldn't see how it made any kind of sense to do without him entirely. Maybe a sliver of Cayo really was better than nothing at all—because nothing else would do. The thought of another man was laughable. What would be the point? Another man wouldn't be Cayo.

Why couldn't they continue as they'd been? She considered it now, scowling fiercely into her sink basin, and the truth was, she couldn't even remember why she'd been so angry with him. Or why she'd been so desperate to get away from him. These weeks were the longest she'd gone without seeing him since she'd started to work for him five years ago. And she hated it. She craved the simple solace of his dark gaze, his impatient voice. Him. She missed *him*.

He might not want her the way she wished he could. He might only have proposed to her as some last-ditch effort to hold on to something he didn't want to lose, the same way he might feel about a particularly limited-edition racecar, for example. Dru understood that. And it wasn't that it didn't hurt. It was that being without him hurt more.

She wanted him more than she wanted her self-respect, it turned out, whatever that made her. A fool. Her mother. A very sad woman destined for a sad life of *slivers*. She supposed she would spend the rest of her life dealing with the fallout of this choice she couldn't seem to help making today. One way or the other.

But in the meantime, she knew exactly what she had to do.

Dru strode back into his life, and into the center of his office, on an otherwise unremarkable Wednesday afternoon.

She looked casual and chic in tight black trousers tucked into high, gleaming boots with dangerous heels and a very complicated sort of burgundy jumper that tied like a scarf and was somehow carelessly elegant. Her glorious hair was swept back into a low ponytail. She'd clearly spent more time in the sun, and it suited her. She had a healthy glow about her, and her eyes were clear as they met his.

Mine, he thought, with a nearly vicious surge of desire.

He wanted his mouth on her. He wanted to be inside her. He wanted her with a savagery that should have taken him out at the knees. Instead, Cayo thrust his hands into his pockets and stood there behind his desk, watching her, as the fury he'd been tamping down began to boil.

"I know how little you like it when people drop in on you without appointments," Dru said in that calm, easy voice of hers that had been haunting him for weeks. "I apologize." She smiled that damned smile of hers. The one he hated. "Your new assistant seems lovely."

"She is perfect in every way," Cayo agreed, his voice all but a growl. "A paragon, in fact. Truly the best personal assistant I've ever had."

"I'm delighted to hear that," she said, so very pleasantly. As if he was just another rich man she had to placate. As if she was working. "Though, if memory serves, you are a bit free with that particular bit of praise. It does render it rather meaningless, I'd say."

He didn't say anything. He couldn't.

"I went back to Bora Bora, as planned," she told him quietly, her gaze searching his, though he didn't know for what.

"I hope your flight was pleasant." He couldn't help his sardonic tone, or the way his brow lifted. "Fly commercial, did you?"

"It took over forty hours." There was the hint of a rueful smile on her lips, which was closer, at least, to something real.

He was meant to respond to that, he knew. He should have. Her eyes met his as if she was encouraging him simply to talk to her, as he might have done before. But he couldn't do it. She'd wrecked him in ways he still didn't understand. She'd left him. He'd let her leave. He still couldn't comprehend either one of those things.

And beyond all that, he wanted her. Pure and simple. Despite knowing exactly how much wanting her destroyed him.

"Dru." He said her name with all the fury and betrayal and longing inside him, letting it pour out of him, not even caring how it hit her. "Why are you here?"

He watched her swallow, hard, as if she was nervous. It became physically painful that he still wasn't touching her.

"I've come to interview," she said, and her voice didn't quite shake but still, he heard emotion there beneath it. A better man might not have taken that as some kind of victory—but he had no such pretensions.

"Interview?" he echoed. He could hear the chill in his own voice. "For what?"

Her chin rose, those gray eyes of hers glittered, and once more, she was hiding from him. He could see it.

"My old position, of course."

He'd dreamed of this. Exactly this. He couldn't help but smile, and he didn't have to see her reaction to know it wasn't a very nice smile at all.

But she didn't break. Not his Dru.

"I'd like my old job back," she said, very distinctly. Politely. She folded her hands in front of her like the passive and obedient underling she had only ever pretended she was, and walked straight into his hands with her head held high. "I've come to beg for it, if necessary."

CHAPTER TEN

HE looked as though he wanted to take her apart with his teeth. Dru fought to control herself—her pounding heart, her galloping pulse, that heaviness in her stomach that couldn't decide if it was desire or anxiety. Or some combination of both.

"If you would like to beg, don't let me stop you," Cayo bit out after a long moment, though his midnight amber eyes gleamed. "You can begin on your knees."

She remembered that day in Bora Bora with picture-perfect clarity. She remembered crawling to him across the polished wood floor, smiling up at him from between his strong legs. Wanting him more than her next breath. She still did. Heat flashed over her, and she was afraid she turned bright red. His eyes were narrow and hot, and she knew beyond a shadow of a doubt that he was remembering the same thing.

"Sweet memories," he said, deliberately provoking her, but she couldn't seem to react the way she might have before. She couldn't seem to breathe past the sheer *force* of him. It was if she'd dulled the intensity of him in her memory, to protect herself. He was shocking and bold, dark gold eyes and jet-black hair, and all that mouthwatering muscle and masculine grace. His suit was perfectly tailored and made him look sleek. Predatory. But not at all tamed. Not Cayo.

And now she knew what he could do with every last inch of that beautiful body. She found she'd lost her voice completely.

His eyes gleamed even more molten gold than before. He stepped out from behind his desk and roamed around to the front, leaning back against it so he was only a foot or two away from her. She schooled herself not to react, not to step away or show anything on her face, even as the back of her neck prickled in warning. In desperate, mindless want.

"Tell me," he said in that soft, supremely dangerous voice of his. "What would possess you to reapply for this job you wanted so desperately to leave? What will it look like the next time you decide you hate me, do you think? What will you throw at me then?"

"Perhaps I was hasty," she managed to say, before she lost what remained of her sense and begged him to take her, however he wanted her. "I may have let my grief over the loss of my brother affect my better judgment."

He eyed her for a long, chilly moment.

"The position is already filled." Cold. Harsh. Absolute. "You were correct," he continued, and there was so much Spanish in his voice that her breath caught. "It was ridiculously easy to replace you. It took a single phone call."

"Oh, I see," she said then, pretending she was as strong as she made herself sound. "You feel I deserve you at your scariest. Vicious and cutting. Is this my latest punishment?"

"What would I possibly punish you for?" he demanded, his voice low and dark. It connected hard with her belly. "It seems that I was nothing more than a convenient way for you to scratch that itch. Just as I told you to do." His smile then should have drawn blood. "What happened, exactly, that I should feel you need punishing?"

Maybe he *had* drawn blood. Maybe this was her, unable to move, bleeding out where she stood and all too aware it was her own fault. She should have left well enough alone. She should have figured out how to survive it—after all, she'd known going into it that getting closer to Cayo would end like this. Exactly like this. Perhaps she shouldn't have been so cavalier.

"Nothing," she said, and it was just as well that she was already so close to numb, already so worn out from all the heartbreak and the grief, that it was only a quiet sort of storm that shook through her then. Only a little bit of rain and another gray sky. No need for any commotion. "Nothing happened at all."

She inclined her head at him and then she turned and started for the door. It had been a mistake to come here. Cayo was a bell that could never be unrung. She had to move on, no matter how much it hurt. In time, she'd recover sufficiently from all of this. Of course she would. She'd stop thinking about him. People recovered from heartbreak all the time, all the world over.

She would, too, she vowed. *She would.*

"There is still one position that remains open, however," he said from behind her, and the dark, almost satisfied tone he used made goose bumps break out all over her skin.

Dru stopped walking, and hated herself for it. *You are no better than a junkie,* her inner voice castigated. *No better than your brother—and just like your mother. You'd take any punishment he doled out.* The masochist inside preened, and she did nothing to prove either one wrong.

"What position is that?" she asked, her voice cool. Disembodied, perhaps, as if she was somewhere else, far from here. Watching from a distance while people other than her were cut to pieces. "Your personal punching bag?"

"My wife."

It was another slap, just as it had been on his island, and this time, she was already so weak. She had already broken down enough to come here. This was just another blow. For a moment she thought she might succumb to the tears that threatened to spill from her eyes—but she blinked them away, furiously, and then turned back to him.

They stared at each other. His dark, wicked brows were raised high, challenge and command. All of the tension and pain, all of the hurt and longing, everything he was to her no matter how she fought against it seemed to hang there and draw tight between them. He looked like thunder. His eyes blazed. And she couldn't seem to summon the pride or self-preservation that might have let her laugh at his twisted version of a proposal. She could only endeavor to keep her tears at bay just a little while longer.

He didn't say that he needed her, that he wanted her. That he longed for *her*. He didn't say that this was hard for him. He looked the way he always looked. Untouchable. Impossibly ruthless. And the most dangerous man she'd ever met.

"Your wife," she said, as if she barely recognized the word. She could hardly speak past the lump in her throat. "And what would that position entail, exactly?"

That predatory gleam shone in his gaze, and his

lean body was so tense, rippling with tension, that she thought he really might pounce. Behind him, rain began to lash at the windows and the sky was dark, and there he stood in the middle of all that, more elemental by far.

"I'm sure we'll think of something," he said, in a voice that made her imagine him thrusting into her: that slick, perfect fit. The electricity. The wildness that made her forget herself completely.

"And when that fades?" she asked, her voice thick. "You are not known for your attention span, are you?"

He pushed away from the desk and started toward her, like a lethal weapon aimed directly at her, and Dru had to fight herself to stand still. Not to run in the opposite direction. Or toward him.

"I have thought of very little else but you since the day you walked in here and quit," he said, moving far too close, forcing her to look up at him. "I never wanted you to leave in the first place. It's not my attention span that's at issue here, is it?"

"I can't marry you." She bit that out, final and sure. Desperate.

His dark brows lowered. "Are you holding out for someone richer, Dru? More powerful?" He didn't laugh as he said it. He didn't have to. His voice dropped, even as his mouth curved into that cold, mocking facsimile of a smile. "Better in bed?"

"Love," she heard herself say, to her utter horror. But there was no unsaying it, even when he looked at her as if she'd thrown another shoe at his head—and had hit her target this time. "There's no point marrying without love."

"Of course," he breathed, and she had never seen that look on his face. Remote and terrible, and if he'd been someone else she'd think she'd ripped his heart from his chest. But this was Cayo. His mouth twisted. "You have already made clear your opinion on my character. Who indeed could marry a monster such as me?"

But though his words were the bitterest she'd ever heard, so much so they made her flinch in reaction, he still moved closer. He reached over and ran his hand down the sleek end of her ponytail, drawing it forward to drape over one shoulder, the gentle touch at odds with the way his gaze burned into hers, fierce and uncompromising. And she remembered, then, that night on the chilly terrace in Milan, when he'd done the same thing. When he'd made her heart ache. When he'd made her believe there was more to this than simply that wild fire.

She remembered treading water in the sea, how she'd ducked under the waves and felt, for a moment, that she might simply let herself sink. How that had seemed better than facing this man who cast such a shadow over her whole life. Who she could not seem to do without, however much she thought she should.

Who had accused her of hiding from him, time and again, and here she was, hiding the most important truth of all from him. When really, what was she protecting? She had nothing and no one. She was wholly alone. She had nothing to lose.

But it was still so hard, so overwhelming, that spots danced before her eyes.

"I don't think you're a monster, Cayo," she whispered. And maybe she had nothing to lose, but it still felt like leaping from a very high cliff into nothingness. "I love you."

He went terrifyingly still, his eyes turning to poured gold.

"And you like to collect things," she continued, not caring about how scratchy her voice sounded, or how many unshed tears pressed against her throat. "You're good at it. You obsess for a time and then you forget all about it while you chase your next obsession." She shook her head, and stepped back from him. "I can't even blame you for that. I saw what your grandfather was like. But how can I marry you when you don't love me back? When you can't?"

"Dru—" he started, but it was a stranger's voice, and he was looking at her as if she'd become a ghost again, right there in front of him, and she knew that it was time to leave. That she should never have come. That she had betrayed herself once again.

"You don't have to say anything," she said softly, and she meant it. She did. "I should have stayed away. I'm sorry."

And then she turned back around and walked away from him. For the last time.

He tracked her back to a converted townhouse in a part of Clapham that was a world away from his three-story penthouse at the top of an old Victorian warehouse perched at the edge of the Thames. This was what she preferred to him, he told himself as he caught the door from one of her neighbors and climbed the narrow, grimy stairs to her second-floor flat—this dingy little place and the dim little life that went with it.

He was so angry with her, Cayo thought it might actually burn off the top of his head.

He pounded on her door, not even pretending to be polite.

"I know you're in there," he growled through the door. "I saw you enter the building not five minutes ago."

He heard the rattle of her locks and then she swung the door open and stood there, scowling up at him, and his curse was that he felt her prettiness like a punch to his gut. Her cheeks were flushed with emotion, making her gray eyes gleam, and he was tired of playing nice. Or trying to. He'd let her go, hadn't he? What else was he meant to do? And she'd been the one to come back and make it perfectly clear that he'd been a fool to do so. That he should have ignored what she'd told him. That he shouldn't have let her go in the first place.

"You are not welcome here," she told him in that cold voice that only made him want her more. It made him think about what best melted all of that ice, and he was certain she could see it on his face when he saw her eyes widen. "Go away."

"I can't do that," he said. He stepped toward her and she leapt back, terrified, he suspected, that he might touch her and prove what a liar she was. He simply shouldered his way inside the flat and kicked the door shut behind him.

And then they were all alone. No brand-new personal assistant in the outer office. And he was blocking the only exit. Cayo could see precisely when that occurred to her, and he smiled.

It was a laughably tiny little place, a bedsit indeed, all in white with a few accent colors—a wooden headboard, the pop of scarlet pillows on her bed—to suggest the idea of space without actually having any. She kept it scrupulously neat, and that was why it seemed slightly bigger than it was—but only slightly.

To his right, a wardrobe and a double bed jutted out

into the small, fitted kitchen. Her laptop lay there, on a café table next to what looked like an abandoned cup of tea, and something about the sight made his chest feel tight. He could imagine her there, dressed in whatever she slept in, her glorious hair knotted on the back of her head as she scrolled through the internet with her morning tea. To his left, when he wrenched his gaze away from her laptop and his imagination, was the smallest version of a living room he'd ever seen, featuring only a plush white armchair, a small trunk and a little shelf with a television sat on it.

This was where she slept. Dreamed. Imagined her life without him. Lived it. Even while claiming she was in love with him.

She would pay for that, too, he promised himself. And dearly.

"This is my space," she fumed at him. "It's not one of the many things that belong to you, that you can storm in and out of as you please. I get to decide what happens here, and I want you to leave."

"I'm not leaving." He leveled a dark look at her. "Nor am I planning to run away if things become intense, unlike some."

He moved farther into the room, grimly amused at the way she skittered away from him, or tried to, as there was nowhere left to go. He picked up one of the handful of framed photographs that sat on the narrow bookshelf at the top of her headboard. A younger Dru and a pale, skinny boy who looked just like her, the same dark hair, those same unfathomable gray eyes. Dru was staring into the camera, mischief in her eyes and a slight smile on her lips, while her brother slung an arm around her neck and laughed. They looked

happy, he thought. Truly happy. The constriction in
his chest pulled taut.

"I did not *run away,*" she was protesting. She
reached over and snatched the picture from his hand,
holding it against her chest for a moment before replac-
ing it. "There was no point continuing that conversation. There still isn't. It hurts too much."

"All you do is run away," he contradicted her, not
even attempting to temper the harshness in his voice.
"You jumped off the damned yacht. You demanded I
let you go. You walked out of my office. And that's
not counting the numerous ways you run away without ever leaving the room."

"That's not running away," she hissed at him.
"That's called the survival instinct. I'll do whatever I
have to do to survive, Cayo, including climb out this
window and down the side of this—"

"I promise you that if you attempt to run away from
me again," he cut her off, his gaze hard on hers, his
voice brooking no argument, "I will lock you up in the
nearest tower and throw away the key."

"Another excellent threat," she retorted, unfazed, if
that glint in her eyes was any indication. "With shades
of Rapunzel, no less. Sadly, not a single one of your
sixteen properties features a tower."

"Then I'll buy one that does."

They glared at each other for a long moment, while
everything inside him rioted. What was it about this
woman? How did she do this to him? Even now, all he
wanted was to sling her over his shoulder and then onto
the bed, and who cared what she thought about that?
He knew how she'd *feel,* and it was rapidly becoming
the only thing that mattered to him. She stood in her
small living area, her arms crossed over her chest, her

sleek boots kicked off next to the armchair so it was
only Dru in her stocking feet with too much color in
her cheeks.

And he wanted her so badly it was painful.

"What do you want, Cayo?" she asked then, her
voice soft, as if it really did hurt her. And he hated that,
but there was no other way.

"I want you," he said, gravely. Deliberately holding her gaze. "That hasn't changed, Dru. I don't believe it will."

She held herself even tighter, while her cheeks paled
and she bit down on her lower lip. And he wanted
his hands on her. He wanted to bury his face in her
hair and inhale the sweet fragrance of it. He wanted
to hold her slender shoulders in his hands. He wanted
to be what chased her pain away, not what caused it.
But he had never known how to do such things. He'd
never tried. He didn't know how to start, and all she
ever did was leave.

But she loved him. And that was like a bright light
where there had never been anything but dark. It was
everything.

"I meant what I said in your office," she whispered.
"I shouldn't have come back. I should have stayed gone.
If you leave now, you'll never see me again."

"I believe you." He kept himself from touching her,
but barely. "But I'm not prepared to watch you martyr
yourself. Not for me."

Dru felt as if he'd kicked her.

"I'm no martyr," she said in a low voice, her mind
reeling.

"Are you certain?" His voice was like silk, danger
and demand. And he didn't back down so much as an

inch. "I can almost see the flames dance around you as you burn yourself at the stake of your choosing."

She couldn't handle this. He was so much larger than life and standing in the middle of her tiny flat, taking it over, as if the space could not contain him. As if it groaned around him, near enough to bursting at the seams with the effort of holding the force of him within these walls. She couldn't seem to make sense of it. Or breathe past the knot in her stomach.

"I have no idea what you're talking about," she said, but she hardly sounded like herself.

He started toward her, backing her up against the cold windows on the far side of the room. It took all of three steps, and then the cold glass was at her back and Cayo was a wall in front of her, big and tempting and more dangerous to her than anything else in the world.

"What have you told yourself?" he asked in that smooth way that made her look around wildly for some escape route. "Have you cried over me, Dru? The man who cannot love you back? Have you forgotten I know you, too?"

"Are you mocking me?" She was incredulous. Not sure if that was anger or agony that surged inside of her, she focused on that fiercely cruel face of his and asked herself why she'd expected anything else. "Are you really that much of a monster, after all?"

His dark amber eyes glowed with something that was not quite malice—something that shivered through her and made her catch her breath. Temper. Fury. And that simmering, unquenchable desire that had ensnared them in this in the first place.

"How convenient for you," he said, his voice no less deadly for all it was so soft, like a lover's. "To find yourself someone else you can love so bravely, and from afar."

His words slammed into her like blows. Dru heard herself make some kind of horrible squeaking sound, and thought her legs would give out. She staggered back against the windowsill, while Cayo only stood there, pitiless, and watched.

"You only love what can never love you back," he told her in that same way, so calmly, as if he didn't know how devastating it was. As if he couldn't see what it was doing to her—or more likely, didn't care. "You arrange your life around distant objects that you can circle but never approach. You thrive on it."

"You…" She could hardly speak. She felt winded. "You don't know what you're talking about."

"Don't I?" She saw the shadows in his eyes, the darkness that lurked there. "Do you love me, Dru? Or do you only think you do because you imagine there's no danger I could ever return it? No chance you might risk yourself, not really. You get to pretend to suffer for your great love while remaining, as ever, completely and utterly alone. Hermetically sealed away. The perfect bloody martyr." He paused, his eyes flashed, and his voice dropped. "Just as you did with your brother."

She lifted a hand as if to stave him off, unable to keep herself from trembling, and sank down against the wall, her legs no longer capable of holding her upright. But he was relentless—he was ruthless down into his bones, and he squatted down before her, his coat flaring around him like a cape, his suit clinging to the hard muscles of his thighs. A perfect and pitiless god, rendering his terrible judgment.

"You," he said, as if she had missed his point, "have no idea what love is."

For what felt like a long time—whole ages, perhaps centuries—Dru could only stare at him, stricken, too deeply shaken even to weep. She felt cracked open, as if she yawned wide and he was the brash, bright light exposing all of her darkness to the air.

And it hurt so much and so deeply that she dimly suspected she hadn't yet got to the real pain—that this was only the shock that preceded it.

"And you do?" she asked eventually. Belligerently, though her voice quaked.

Cayo's eyes were brilliant. Dark and gold and molten fire, burning her alive. He reached over and took her hands in his, and she should have jerked away. But instead, she exulted in the feel of his skin against hers after all this time. It pumped through her like heat, as though her own blood betrayed her, as though there was no part of her that wasn't his no matter what she told herself. Or told him.

"Let me tell you what I know," he told her, his voice low, intense. Urgent. His accent was thick and melodic then, wrapping around her, caressing her. "I want you. I want you in ways that I don't understand. I can live without you, but I don't want to. I don't see the point."

"Cayo—"

"Callate," he ordered her. He shifted back on his heels, dropping her hands though she still felt as if he touched her, as if he surrounded her. She folded her hands over what was left of his heat. "I tried. I let you go. *You came back."* His fierce face looked almost harsh. Stark and serious. "You only love what you cannot have, and I have never been anything but a monster. I've never wanted to be anything but what

I am." His cruel mouth moved slightly, hinting at that curve. "Until now."

Something swelled up in the space between them, precarious and new. Dru felt the tears trickle down her cheeks but made no move to wipe them away. She could only see Cayo. And like one of those hummingbirds that Dominic had inked into his skin, she felt something flutter up and hover, skittish and shy, like some kind of gift. *Hope,* she thought, and that great cavern inside her, that terrible emptiness that had eaten her alive for so long, began at last to shrink.

She didn't want pain. She didn't want that masochistic streak. She wanted him. She always had. And she was tired of hiding. It was time to stop. Past time.

This time she was the one who reached out. She sat forward and ran her hands along his severe jaw, then held his fierce, impossible face between her hands. She felt the heat of him moving through her, warming her from the inside out.

"If I am not a martyr," she said, her voice small but strong, "and you are not a monster, then who do you suppose we are?"

"That's the point," he said, his hands coming up to cover hers, his gaze melting into hers, the world shifting all around them and the fire that always burned between them bright and hot and true. Making them something more than they were before. Soldering them together. Welding them, finally, into one. Not clay, but tempered steel. "I want to find out. With you."

"I think we can do that," she whispered, and then she tipped forward and kissed him, like a vow.

He found her sprawled out on one of the loungers on the private deck off the owner's suite on the great yacht, her lovely curves displayed to mouthwatering perfection in a wickedly simple bikini.

She smiled as he approached, but did not set aside her tablet until he lifted her bodily into the air and captured her mouth with his. He had not seen her in almost a full twenty-four hours and felt as desperate as if it had been years.

He set her to her feet carefully, enjoying the slide of her against him.

"What is it?" she asked, her clever eyes moving over his face.

He reached into his pocket and pulled out a long, narrow white box and handed it to her. She looked up at him for a moment, then looked down and opened the box. She gasped. And Cayo tensed, not certain this had been the right thing to do.

Dru pulled the pendant into the air and stared at it, her eyes filling with tears.

"Hummingbirds..." she whispered. Two birds nestled together on the silver chain, in the bright and bold colors that could only be Murano glass. They sparkled in the golden sunlight, looking very nearly alive. And when she looked at him again, her eyes were wet, but she was smiling.

"You won't forget him," Cayo said, his voice rough. "And neither will I."

She threw her arms around him and kissed him then. For a long time. Soft and sweet. Making both of them sigh.

It had been eight months now since that scene in her cramped Clapham bedsit. Eight months of Dru in his life, testing him and changing him, making him wonder how he'd lived without her for so long. He could no longer imagine any possible scenario that did not include this woman, who had somehow made him the man he'd never believed he could be. Flesh and blood. Alive. Not a monster, after all. Not as long as she loved him.

"When are you going to marry me?" he demanded when they were both breathless and she was boneless against him.

"When you deserve it," she said, pulling away from him. She wiped at her eyes and then she looked at him as if she thought that eventuality was highly unlikely, and he laughed.

"Must I bribe you into it?" he asked. "You won't take a house. Land. Atolls or islands."

He waved a hand and she followed the gesture, looking out over the deep blue of the Aegean Sea toward the sunny, green little island that stretched there off the side of the yacht. Private and uninhabited. And his. She had insisted that he visit all of his properties or sell them, and so he had, leaving the minutia of his affairs more and more in the capable hands of his fleet of vice presidents. *Delegating.* This Greek island, one of the Cyclades not far from Mykonos, was the last on the list. He found he liked it. And the process of exploring them all, with her.

"No," she agreed. "I don't want your property. But…"

"Yes?" She amused him. Fascinated him.

"Perhaps a company." Her gray eyes gleamed as she fastened the pendant around her neck. The hummingbirds seemed to dance and shimmer against her skin. "Just a small one."

"Why am I unsurprised that the life of leisure bores you?"

She only smiled. "You have that boutique advertising agency in New York, don't you, that is currently in dire need of leadership?"

He was aware she knew full well that he did.

"What do you know about managing an advertising agency?" But his tone was indulgent and in any case, he had no doubt that this woman could do anything she chose to do, and well.

"I managed you for five years," she said dryly. "I imagine a company filled with artistic Americans could only be a breeze in comparison. A bit of holiday, really."

"I love you," he said, because he did, and because he could think of nothing that pleased him more than the idea of her doing this *with* him. Building all of this *with* him. Making it their empire, not his. Making it matter. "You can run whatever you want, *mi amor*. But I will have to insist that you marry me."

She only watched him, her gray eyes clear and sparkling, and he reached over to take her hands in his, pulling her to him. The sun spilled all over her, bathing her in light, and still she shone brighter.

"There is a little-known clause in all my contracts," he said softly, pressing kisses to her cheek, to the freckles across her nose, to her sweet mouth. "All Vila Group subsidiaries must be run by a Vila. So you see how it is. My hands are tied."

Dru laughed and threaded her arms around his neck.

"You know how I love a sacrifice," she teased him. "I suppose it's a good thing, then, that I love you enough to make such a huge one."

"It is," he said gruffly, but he smiled, and then kissed her again, sealing it.

And it would be, he thought. A very good thing,

and they would spend their whole lives making it better. He had no doubts.

He was Cayo Vila. He didn't take no for an answer, and he didn't know how to fail.

* * * * *

So you think you can write?

It's your turn!

Mills & Boon® and Harlequin® have joined forces in a global search for new authors and now it's time for YOU to vote on the best stories.

It is our biggest contest ever—the prize is to be published by the world's leader in romance fiction.

And the most important judge of what makes a great new story?

YOU—our reader.

Read first chapters and story synopses for all our entries at
www.soyouthinkyoucanwrite.com

Vote now at www.soyouthinkyoucanwrite.com!

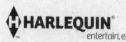

HARLEQUIN®
entertain, enrich, inspire™

MILLS & BOON®

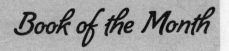

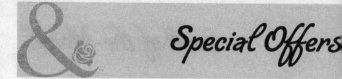

Have Your Say

A

You've just finished your book.
So what did you think?

We'd love to hear your thoughts on our
'Have your say' online panel
www.millsandboon.co.uk/haveyoursay

- 🌹 Easy to use
- 🌹 Short questionnaire
- 🌹 Chance to win Mills & Boon®
  goodies